A LAINEY MAYNARD MYSTERY

The Family Tree Murders

LAURA HERN

Cover Design/Interior Design: Linda Boulanger

ISBN: 978-1-6175-2208-6

Contents

Thank You

Thank you for supporting authors by buying, reading, and reviewing our books. I give you my utmost gratitude! I couldn't continue to tell stories if it weren't for you and for the support team that surrounds me!

Social Media

Laura Hern Social
Website & Newsletter:
https://www.laurahern.com

Facebook:
https://www.facebook.com/laurahernauthor

Also in series:
Murder In The Backwater
Curtain Call At Brooksey's Playhouse
Christmas Corpse At Caribou Cabin
And more coming soon!

Praise and Reviews

"A quirky yet brilliant detective."

"Nothing beats an easy read by the pool or beach, but this book adds a delightful level of quirkiness with the murder mystery being solved. Lainey is a clever and hardworking detective, ready to tackle an unusual mystery involving DNA testing. The twists within the mystery are perfect and I was on the edge of my seat to see how the story came out." *Jimmy B*

"Excellent!!"

"Another great little murder solved by Lainey Maynard and her fun group of friends! This was a fun adventure when a body was found during the preparations for a big town celebration. Super sleuth, Lainey sets out to

solve this murder. Chaos ensues! It's delightful. I love
this light hearted and fun series."

W. B. Barker

"Fun, light, quick moving and well written!"
"What a pleasure it was to read this book!! I loved the
main character, Lainey Maynard, with all her little
oddities and quirks. This author has created a group of
likable and fun loving people who just happen to get
involved in a serious claim of murder and mayhem by
some very devious relatives. DNA testing is involved.
Who you are related to could get you killed. The
method of these ugly murders is very sneaky and I
would have never suspected it. The investigation and
result make you want to read more! I have signed up
for her newsletter and anxiously await more in this
series!"

Karla Kay

Introduction

Lainey Maynard thought DNA testing websites, promising the chance to find long lost or unknown relatives and the current fad around the world, were a huge waste of time and would vanish as quickly as fidget spinners, twerking, and the ice bucket challenge.

Little did she know that a string of DNA, spilled coffee, a handsome businessman, family inheritances, suspicions of murder, stolen evidence, and body bags would bring deadly consequences her way. She is cunning, brave, intelligent, and a seasoned investigator, but will she need more than her intuition and wit to survive?

Chapter One

"Brrrr...this dismal snow and sleet have to end soon, right?" Lainey thought aloud as she peered through her smudged windshield. "Why can't wiper blades last forever?" She turned her radio from the depressing weather forecast back to the audiobook she had been listening to.

Lainey Maynard worked as a fraud investigator for a large insurance company and had clients in a seven-state area. She worked from home in a small bedroom she'd turned into her office. With the constantly new and improved advanced computer technology, she could do much of the research needed for a case from her ergonomic home office chair. However, she traveled by car most of the time to gather information.

After years on the road and hearing the same songs over and over again, she finally decided to bite the bullet and buy audiobooks. Even as a child, she loved the old-fashioned murder mysteries. She rarely had time these days to watch the British television mystery series she always enjoyed. At least if she had to drive for hours, listening to audiobooks helped pass the time.

Moving to Minnesota from Texas some dozen years ago, Lainey still dreaded the very long winters. Her favorite word to describe those dreary winter days was 'Yucky!'

Pulling into one of her favorite coffee shop bookstores to get a non-fat mocha Frappuccino, a spinach pretzel with marinara sauce, and the books she had ordered, Lainey hurried through the checkout. She paid the cashier, bundled up her bags, and headed for the store exit. The Whoopee group was meeting for dinner tonight and she still had a two-hour drive ahead of her.

Her hands were so full she had backed into the outside door to open it and bumped into a person who was trying to get in the door just as quickly.

"Oh! I am so sorry!" Lainey exclaimed as she bent down to pick up her books that were now drenched in her spilled Frappuccino. She looked up to see a middle-aged man also covered in her coffee and looking not a bit pleased.

The man bristled, not offering to help her, and in a deep baritone voice grunted. "Look, sweetheart, we're all in a hurry. Why don't you be more careful, honey?"

He cleared his throat as he stepped on what was going to be her spinach pretzel.

"Sweetheart?" Lainey stood up as flames of fire were beginning to burn in her dark brown eyes. Lainey, 5' 4" tall and of slight build, was glaring upward at the very tall man in front of her. "Honey?" she repeated. She took a brief moment and purposely looked at him from head to toe. He appeared to be a well-dressed, successful businessman. His salt and pepper hair was styled with not a strand out of place. The beige overcoat he wore with the collar turned up and a plaid scarf neatly stuffed inside, reminded Lainey of an 80's cartoon detective her kids had watched on television.

"You appear to be a nice, fairly handsome man that may have women with panting hearts waiting to comfort your every whim, but I don't know you from Adam," Lainey stated as politely as possible. "My name is not 'sweetheart' or 'honey' and I apologize for bumping into you."

She picked up her things while he stood there looking at her, bored and unamused. Her pretzel was still firmly squished under his foot. "Excuse me," she said as she stood up. "I have to be going. Here's the marinara sauce for your pretzel. Have a great day... honey!" She stated as she tossed the sauce packet at him and walked over to her car, smiling to herself.

Lainey was on the freeway slowly making her way

back to Mirror Falls when her Bluetooth signaled an incoming call. The caller ID indicated it was Francy.

"Hey, Lainey! Are you going to make it to dinner tonight?" Francine Baines, otherwise known to her friends as Francy, was one of the four ladies that had started meeting together twice a month several years ago.

"Hello, Francy! Yep. I'm doing my best to get there by 5:30. We are meeting for cards afterward, right? Do you want me to bring treats?"

"Nope. Mom has treats ready when we play cards at her house after supper. Remember it's the Chinese place tonight. See you soon!"

Lainey hit the call end button and focused on the boring drive ahead of her.

She enjoyed being a part of this group. At first, the four ladies met because they had something in common. They were widows. Except for Francy, who came only to support her mother, Vera. Over the years, the group had become much more than friends. They were family to each other!

Vera Abernathy took over the role of 'Mom' for the group. Her husband had been a loved and respected local doctor and she had worked with him for years. Being the oldest of the four ladies, Vera had more energy and get-up-and-go than a person half her age!

Francine Baines was Vera's only daughter. Francy had worked as a police dispatcher for more than 30 years and was happily enjoying semi-retirement with her husband, Roger. In the warmer months, Tuesday evenings were reserved for rides with the Harley Motorcycle club. In the winter, Tuesday nights meant you could find Roger playing Bingo at the local VFW. Sometimes, Francy tagged along and took great joy on those rare occasions when she was the big game winner. She collected anything: greeting cards, statues, figurines, pictures, and jewelry. If it had a buffalo on it, she loved it.

And then there was the bubbly Della Kristiansen. In fact, it was Della that inadvertently created the name of the group. At heart, she was a genealogist and loved history, but reality was a different story. She had worked as the production manager for a soybean manufacturer for years. She retired and moved to Mirror Falls to marry the local mortician.

Growing up with five much older brothers and being the only girl in her family, she could be one tough cookie if needed. Della would pop in at the dinner meeting greeting everyone with a 'Whoop, whoop, whoop!' And so, the name Whoopee group stuck. Restaurants got to know the women and greeted them as the Whoopee group. One local eatery always had a table waiting for them.

Playing cards was an absolute must after every Whoopee dinner meeting. While they visited about current life happenings, they played cards or dice games. Arguably the most important part of the evening...treats! Nuts or cookies or bars, and always something chocolate. Many times, new recipes were tested on the group. And, of course, there was coffee. Lots and lots of coffee! The talk this evening had turned to the recent fad about requesting a DNA family history.

"My gosh," Francy began, "All I see on TV are ads for DNA kits. Order this and find your heritage, or find relatives you don't know about, or get your health predictions!" She chuckled and added, "Who needs more relatives or health issues to worry about?"

Vera nodded. "We have a long history and by golly no one is going to get my DNA!" she declared. The group laughed together.

"I have some reservations about sending off anything unique about me. After all, is the world really ready for another Lainey Maynard?"

"I don't know," Della giggled. "I think it might be fun to have a twin. I want to know if they can reprogram my genes. You know, the ones that force me to eat more chocolate and pistachios!"

"Didn't you have a friend whose aunt or uncle did this DNA kit testing? Weren't they startled or mad or surprised by the results?" Vera asked, patting Francy on the shoulder.

"Come to think of it one of my high school friends

was saying something about that." Francy frowned, took her phone and clicked on her social media link.

"In fact, I think several of her cousins or in-laws did the testing, too. If I remember correctly, the family was shocked that the tests showed some of the siblings were not actually from the same parents."

"Oops! Bet that was a surprise!" Della smiled. "Nothing like learning about the skeletons in your closet! It depends on how accurate a person thinks those tests are, I guess."

"I think the health testing showed a high likelihood that family members would develop cancer. No, wait, it was a likelihood they would die from heart disease or heart attack," Francy commented and turned off her phone.

"I'm out!" Vera raised her hands. "Count up your points, girls! Have time for one more hand? We have to finish these cookies and candy tonight."

While Vera shuffled the cards, Lainey put the last ginger cookie on her napkin. "Several of the adoption sites encourage adoptees to do these DNA searches. I've had emails and ads sent to me for years."

"Ever thought of doing that, Lainey?" Della asked.

"Nope. I was adopted at five days old and my parents were the greatest gift God could give me. They were there when I was sick, had a bad dream, at my proudest moments, and my saddest moments. I have no desire to locate people who did the best possible for me at the time by giving me up for adoption. I'm not saying DNA testing is good or bad. It's just not for me." Lainey picked up her cards and looked at the others.

Vera carefully adjusted the four cards in her hand and surveyed those on the table. "Well, you never know. If you don't know your bloodline and want to find out, I guess it would be the thing to do."

"Maybe," mused Lainey. "Someone else can do this research. I'm swamped at work with my own cases."

Della suddenly shouted, "Dang it, Francy! You can't go out in the first round! I haven't drawn a card yet!"

"Read'em and weep!" Francy giggled. "I believe it's called Gin."

The ladies laughed, finished off the dark chocolate covered raisins, and went home.

Lainey woke up the next morning with Powie, her cat, purring loudly while he positioned his backside directly in front of her nose. That was the sign that he was hungry, and it occurred at 4 a.m. every morning.

"Okay, let's get you some food." Lainey sat up, put on her snuggly socks, and looked around for her cell phone and glasses. "Thank goodness I'm a light sleeper, Powie. But can't we change your clock to maybe 4:30 for once?" She smiled as she picked up the purring black fur ball, scratched his back, and put him down at his food dish.

She turned on the TV and the coffee maker, then looked at her cell phone. "Why am I still getting all these spam emails?" She muttered. "I spend more time blocking emails than writing emails!" Lainey saw that among her regular email was one that was marked 'urgent – Francy's friend.'

The email was from a Mary Chase, a friend of Francy's, who needed to meet today at 1 p.m. at Babe's House of Caffeine. The email stated it was about some family issue and very important to meet as soon as possible.

She replied to the email and put on her calendar the 1 p.m. appointment. She wondered if it was about fraud or hiring her company for something else. Either way, she looked forward to sipping a Babe's strong mocha Frappuccino — no whip, of course!

Lainey arrived about fifteen minutes early for her meeting with Mary Chase. She was known for being early. She felt better prepared when she was early.

Babe's House of Caffeine was a 1930's home that had been renovated years ago into a 70's-type coffeehouse complete with black lights across the ordering bar, a strobe light hanging from the ceiling beam that hadn't worked in years, and a slightly musty odor of dirty socks. The old hardwood floors creaked when you walked across them.

The place reminded Lainey of a little garage hangout she and her school friends frequented. She grew up in a tiny town and the dad of one of her friends had let them paint the inside walls of their storage garage with psychedelic pink, green, and yellow. They usually had to move the lawnmower into the yard before putting up lawn chairs when they met so they could visit and enjoy their sack lunches and colas. Her mom called it a hippie shack. She chuckled at the memory.

Lainey walked to the back of the room and sat at a table facing the front door. This would eliminate the element of surprise is someone should come up behind her. She didn't know what Mary Chase looked like and this would give her ample time to check out everyone who came in the coffee shop.

Her phone alarm vibrated letting her know it was 1 p.m. Lainey was waiting to order coffee in case Mary wanted something. She was turning off her phone when she noticed a woman walk through the door, her expression confused and worried.

The woman, hurriedly pulled off her coat and scarf, looking from table to table. Lainey waived and stood up to greet her when she reached the table.

"I'm Lainey Maynard. Can I help you find someone?" Lainey had learned not to mention other people by name until she was certain it was the correct person.

"Yes, I'm Mary Chase," the tall, and a bit rumpled, redhead replied as she shook Lainey's hand. "Thank you for meeting with me."

"Not a problem. Have a seat. Can I order you a coffee or something?"

She ordered two coffees and waters and waited for Mary to get settled in her chair before starting a conversation. She noticed Mary's coat was a black down-filled waist jacket with a blazing red plaid scarf. Mary straightened her blue reindeer-covered sweater before sitting down. Lainey's first impression of Mary was that she was a nice, down to earth person.

"I see you are friends with Francy," Lainey began, hoping it would allow Mary to open up.

"Yes, we went to the same high school. I think you are an investigator or something, right? I hope you can help me. I can't afford an attorney." Mary nervously rolled the edge of the small napkin under the coffee cup.

A hundred things ran through Lainey's mind. Investigator, nervous, can't afford legal fees. Her years on the job had trained her to listen and then think before responding to anything.

"Mary, I am not an attorney, nor can I give you legal advice. I'm sorry if that is why you are here," she stated.

"Oh no! That's not what I mean at all!" Mary looked up, her big green eyes a little bit misty. Mary must be in her 40's, but at the moment, she looked like a scared young girl.

"A few years ago, my sister, brother, and I thought it

would be fun to send our DNA off to find our long, lost ancestors. Everyone was talking about how fun it was to find relatives or cousins they'd never heard about. We sent in our little spit samples thinking it would be fun if we turned out to be related to some famous person. It was only for fun." She stared at her coffee cup.

"I've heard of these kits, Mary, but I haven't personally had any experience with them. How do you think I can help you?"

"My brother had different results from my sister and me," she said flatly. "Seems he had a different mother than we did."

"Oh," Lainey said. "That must have been a shock."

"Yes. At first we figured it must be a mistake. You know, someone entered a wrong mother, father or data or something." Mary blew on her coffee and then took a big sip. "But it was true."

Lainey was silent waiting for her to continue. She still couldn't picture why Mary was telling her this.

"Long story short, I'm sure you are wondering how this affects our meeting." It was as if Mary had read Lainey's thoughts. "I've spent a lot of time researching my brother's new family line," Mary paused, looked briefly behind her, and whispered. "I think his family is being murdered and I am afraid for him."

Lainey's mouth dropped open for a second. She leaned forward in her chair and whispered.

"Murdered? Why would you think they are being murdered?"

Lainey regretted the comment as soon as it popped out of her mouth. She was sure Mary saw the shock and disbelief on her face.

"You don't believe me," Mary sighed. "My brother doesn't believe me either. It's okay." She stood up to leave.

"Wait! Please, don't leave. I apologize for my comment. I wasn't expecting to hear what you said. Please, sit down and tell me why you think this."

There was a noticeable, awkward pause as Mary sat down. She took a minute to gather her thoughts and continued.

"You are a researcher or investigator, aren't you?"

"Yes, we investigate insurance fraud of different types," Lainey answered.

"But you know people who have connections to find out things, right? I'm afraid my brother is going to die, and no one will help me!" Tears began to fill her hauntingly green eyes. She was serious.

Lainey sat back in her chair and took a moment before responding. "I'm still not quite sure what you want me to do. What proof do you have? Maybe you should be talking to the police."

"The police won't help. I tried to explain it to them. They said DNA research was not enough to go on."

Lainey needed more information. "Tell me the details about why you feel your brother is in danger."

Over the next thirty minutes, Mary explained that while searching this new family tree line, she found birth and death records with names and dates going back a few generations. She had noticed that very recently, two of the known bloodline brothers had died unexpectedly. In fact, if the recorded information was correct, only her brother and one other relative remained alive.

Lainey listened while Mary spoke. Thoughts were swirling in her mind. People die, bloodlines die out. What was the origin of this new bloodline? Wealth? Blue Collar? Immigrant? What makes her think of murder?

Mary finished by telling Lainey that she'd researched sites that were used to identify bodies, DNA, and criminal activities. "I think many of these relatives died in suspicious ways."

Lainey's ears perked up. "You can access a database like that?"

"Yes."

"Wow. I had no idea people could get to that kind of information. Do you have a CD or paper files of these results? Remember," she added, "I'm not an attorney or police officer."

"I have a ton of information. Can we meet at my house where I have access to my computer?"

"You bet," Lainey replied as she opened her phone calendar.

"I don't want legal or police action here. Sometimes it even sounds ridiculously far-fetched to me," Mary admitted.

They decided to meet on the coming Saturday and Lainey entered the information onto her calendar.

Chapter Two

After a extremely busy week, Saturday finally arrived. Usually, Saturday mornings were spent doing the chores she put off during the week. Laundry, cleaning, and dusting were not her most favorite things, but Lainey had learned long ago she was a morning person. If she was going to get these done, she had to get started early. As she completed her chores, she thought of her upcoming meeting with Mary Chase.

By 2 p.m., Lainey was standing on the porch of a small, white farmhouse with a burned-wooden sign across the top of the front door with the words "The Chase House." She saw duct tape across the doorbell and decided to knock.

Mary Chase opened the door, smiled, and greeted

her. "Hi, Lainey. I didn't know if you would come. I've got everything ready. Please, make yourself at home."

She nodded, thanked her, and stepped inside. Two large poodles greeted her, tails wagging as they jumped on her legs.

"Millie! Gertie! Stop that!" Mary shooed the dogs away. "I'm sorry about that. The girls are really friendly. Please follow me into the kitchen."

"No problem. I have a cat that wants to be in your lap constantly."

"Put your things on the table if you can find a space. Nothing can hurt this old thing. It's the only desk I have and I use it for everything." Mary pulled back a chair.

She was right. There was a laptop, several piles of papers, mail, a bag of doggie treats, a yoga video, and two used candles on the table. Lainey sat and gently pushed a couple of piles of papers to her left to make room for her laptop and a yellow legal pad for notes.

"Thank you for seeing me, Mary. I know Saturdays must be busy for you."

"We're farmers, so the work here never ends." Mary turned on her laptop and handed a larger manila file to Lainey. "I didn't know where to start, so here is what I have."

Lainey opened the file. Inside were handwritten notes, printed papers, some sort of maps or drawings, and blurry reprinted receipts or something. *This is going to take some time.*

"My goodness, Mary, this is a lot of information! Where did you find all this?"

"I started digging after our DNA results showed my brother, Douglas Reynolds, had a different mother than my sister and me." She stood and grabbed a pot of coffee that had been heating on the stove. She also brought two coffee cups with a tractor stenciled on the front and the words Farmers Do It Best below it.

"Coffee?" Mary asked.

"Yes, please. Would you happen to have any coffee goop?" Lainey said without thinking. Noticing the puzzled look on Mary's face, she backtracked. "Oh! I'm sorry! Cream and sugar are what I call coffee goop."

Mary handed her another cup filled with sugar and creamer packets. "Doug thinks this is silly, that I'm imagining all this. But it's all here, plain as day."

"This is a lot of information. Can you give me a summary or something before I dig into all of this?" Lainey asked, picking up her legal pad to make notes.

"DNA researching is big on learning about family trees. You know, a chart showing generations of mothers, fathers, siblings, your weird Uncle Ed..." Mary turned her laptop around to show Lainey her family tree.

"My mother was Harriet Evans Reynolds. She and my dad, DeWayne, had three kids: Ann, my brother, Doug, and me."

"Okay." Lainey wrote down the names. "Can I take a picture of this screen? It will be easier for me than trying to write all of this down again."

Mary agreed and continued with the conversation. "When our DNA tests came back, Doug's listed our mom as his stepmother. We didn't believe it at first but have since confirmed that through one of Dad's living relatives. It was a one-night stand kind of thing my Dad had right out of high school that happened a few weeks before he met my mother. The baby was born and left in my dad's car one night. I guess the lady never told Dad or anyone. Dad told Mom and they raised the boy, my brother Doug, as their own."

"Wow. What is the name of this one-night stand woman?"

Mary scrolled down her screen to a separate family tree chart. "Stella Baxter Sullivan."

Lainey leaned closer, putting her reading glasses higher up on her nose as she examined the screen. She noticed a line marrying Stella Baxter to William Sullivan and four children under their names. None of them were named Douglas Reynolds.

"There seems to be four children by Stella and William. Looks like three of them are deceased. The only child living is a Raymond Baxter Sullivan. But I don't see your brother Doug on here."

"He's not listed because he wouldn't let us put him in there." She went on to say that members of these DNA ancestry registries share information with each other. Names and entire family trees can be added by anyone.

"One big reason for using these sites is that your results can be shared throughout the world based on similar DNA traits. It would be impossible to gather all this information on your own," Mary explained.

"You mean that anyone can look at your DNA results?"

"Yes, but only if you have given them permission."

Lainey sat back, sipped her lukewarm coffee, and thought for a minute, still trying to get an understanding of how all of this was adding up to murder.

"I still don't see how this tree chart tells you someone is murdering people or how your brother is in danger." She was hoping Mary had proof of some kind and that this was not a waste of time.

Mary looked at her for several minutes, got up, and walked over to the refrigerator. On top was a set of three metal canisters of decreasing size, decorated with chickens. She took the middle one down and came back to the table.

"These were my mother's pride and joy," she commented, smiling as she pulled open the old metal lid carefully. "My family knows that no one touches these but me."

Gently, Mary lifted out a small sandwich baggie with something black inside it. She sat down the canister and handed Lainey the baggie. Lainey's curiosity was on high alert as she opened it to find a jump drive.

"You have information saved on this jump drive about the possible murder?" Lainey asked anxiously.

Mary lowered her voice and said, "I've saved a lot of files that I think proves someone is murdering the Sullivan family bloodline. I took this information to the police station, but they told me DNA research results were not proof enough that murder had been committed."

Lainey didn't know if Mary was disgusted, disgruntled, or simply tired of explaining her theories.

"When we talked earlier this week, you mentioned you had proof from a database used in criminal investigations." Lainey started to plug the jump drive into her laptop.

"Wait! Don't install that here! Take it with you!" Mary instructed in a somewhat panicked voice. Lainey quickly put the drive back into the baggie and tucked it into her fanny pack.

"I'm sorry, but I think you need to study that at your home." She was looking toward the back door. "My brother is coming over for supper soon and I don't want to upset him."

"I will do that." Lainey replied. "What database did you…" she was interrupted before she could finish her sentence.

"Oh, it's all there." Mary added standing up. "Doug will be here any minute. You need to go now. Please call me later?"

"Of course! Thank you for taking the time to see me today. I look forward to talking with you soon!"

Lainey gathered her things, walked out the front door, got back in her car and headed for home. *Something is going on with Mary and brother Doug.*

"Why is this little jump drive so important?" Lainey stated out loud. Knowing she might have a long evening ahead, she decided to get a skinny mocha Frappuccino to keep her alert.

"Hello, Lainey!" A cheery voice greeted in the drive-through speaker.

"How did you know it was me?"

"We have a camera on the speaker so we see you, but you can't see us!" The young lady giggled. "Want a medium nonfat mocha Frap to go? No whip?"

"Yes, please!"

I come here way too often. She thought to herself,

looking in the rearview mirror. "Holy cow!" She muttered out loud. "Really? Am I getting a double chin?"

She paid for the coffee, took a quick sip, and drove the rest of the way home. Lainey hurried into the house, sat down at her work desk, and dug out the baggie with the jump drive from her fanny pack. She loved the old roll-top desk that her dad had bought at some garage or estate sale years ago. It wasn't the most comfortable desk, nor did it have a large desktop area. It was weathered by use and the roll-top no longer rolled up or down, but she could still see her dad sitting at the desk working or reading when she came home from school every day. That made her feel close to him.

"Twenty years and I still miss you, Dad." Lainey sighed as she turned on her wireless keyboard. Even as a young girl, Lainey was a thinker and often talked out loud or to herself when she was confused or needed to think things through. Her dad used to say, "When Lainey mumbles to herself, better watch out and move out of the way. She has figured something out!"

She put her drink on the coaster next to the keyboard. "Okay ," she said as she inserted the drive into her MAC big screen monitor. "Show me what you've got."

Lainey sat back in her chair waiting for the

contents to appear on the screen. She didn't know what to expect and was ready for many files or folders to pop up. She was pleasantly surprised that only two folders appeared. One was tagged Gen and the other Murder.

She quickly opened the Murder folder. There were four files listed: Karl Sullivan, deceased; Eugene Sullivan, deceased; Harold Sullivan, deceased; and Raymond Sullivan. They were the children of Stella Baxter and William Sullivan that Lainey saw on Mary's computer screen.

More intrigued than ever, she clicked on the file for Raymond Sullivan, thinking he might still be alive. As she reached over to take a sip of her coffee, a large picture filled the screen. Lainey gasped in disbelief dropping her drink all over herself.

"Well, poop!" She moaned as she took a closer look at the picture. In full color, staring directly at her was the arrogant, salt and pepper-haired man she had bumped into and spilled coffee on last week.

"What! I can't believe it!" She cried out as she grabbed the tissue box on the desk and tossed the now empty cup into the trash. "This guy made me spill my coffee... again!"

Lainey stared at the picture. It was a recent photo taken from an office. The floor to ceiling windows behind Raymond's silhouette displayed a nighttime city skyline of Minneapolis that she recognized immediately. It was an area between the Stone Arch Bridge and Boom Island Park showcasing the bridge, the lights of the tall buildings, and the Mississippi River.

"This office view must have cost you a pretty penny, Raymond." She clicked on the information tab listed below the photo. Several file names appeared.

"I wonder if Mary added these files." Lainey opened the file marked 'Known Background.'

As she began reading the information, she opened her Mac Notes file and began copying. Raymond Baxter Sullivan, fourth of four sons, born to Stella Baxter and William Sullivan. Written in bold print and underlined, the next line read: son and only living heir of Sullivan's Best Poultry empire.

Lainey abruptly stopped reading. The Sullivan family was well-known throughout Minnesota, and Sullivan's Best Poultry was one of the largest poultry operations in the United States.

She googled William Sullivan and found that he was considered to be a hard-working, ambitious man with self-taught business savvy. He began as a small turkey farmer. His determination, grit, and sometimes harsh or unethical business tactics had grown the company to include a dozen turkey processing plants, an army of poultry farmers to purchase from, a fleet of truck drivers who delivered their products, and several small retail outlets in the Minneapolis area.

Lainey thought aloud, "William most certainly made a few enemies while building his business. Did he make someone mad enough to commit murder?" She continued copying the information into her notes.

She returned back to Raymond's file. "Raymond was born in 1965 and is now running the poultry empire," She read aloud. That was the only other entry under his name. She closed the file and clicked on each of the other files. As she read each sibling's information, she copied it into her notes file.

Karl Sullivan, stillborn in 1958. *No murder committed here.*

Eugene Sullivan, born 1960 and died in 2017. There was an attachment under this name. It stated he died in a car accident on Highway 12. No autopsy was performed, and it was claimed an accidental death.

Lainey continued on to Harold Sullivan and silently read his information. He was born in 1962 and had died in early 2017 in a fish house accident. She knew ice fishing was common in the winter months and that at times accidents had occurred, but she needed more details. The entry stated no autopsy was performed.

Her over-active mind went to the thought that it could be accidental death from carbon monoxide poisoning. She closed the file and sat back in her chair to think, still trying to get a clear picture of what Mary Chase was hoping to prove. Questions were swirling around in her head. Did Mary think Eugene and Harold Sullivan were murdered and it was covered up? Did she think Raymond and Doug were next on the murderer's list? And how did she know that no autopsies were performed?

Before emailing Mary to set up another meeting, Lainey wanted to review the other folder marked 'history.' Clicking open the link, she saw a listing of three people, Doug Reynolds, Mary Reynolds Chase, and Ann Reynolds. Beside each name were paragraphs about each person.

Lainey made a note to herself to ask Mary if she had been the one who created the file because the fonts of the paragraphs changed several times.

She began reading the paragraph about Doug… "The oldest, born in 1955 and never married. Doug quit high school after the accident with Dad. He took over the farm at age 17…"

Lainey highlighted this, making a note to herself to ask Mary about the accident as she continued reading. "…Struggles to make ends meet on the farm and works part-time as a body driver for the county and funeral homes. Still takes care of Ann…"

Was Doug angry about having to run the farm at such an early age? Why was he taking care of Ann? Where have I heard of body drivers?

She glanced down at the next paragraph which was about Mary.

"Mary, the middle child born in 1961, was the smartest…"

Lainey giggled. "If you wrote this, good for you, Mary!" She continued reading.

"…She helped on the farm until she married her own farmer in 1982. She has three children, none are named Ann."

None of them named Ann? Why did she feel that was important? Does she get along with Ann?

Curiously, she scrolled down to the last paragraph with Ann's information.

"Ann, the baby of the family, born in 1965. Born with her left leg much shorter than the right. Dad blamed Mom and made wooden canes for Ann to use…"

Lainey raised her eyebrow. Her interest piqued, she leaned forward and continued reading.

"…Always tagged along behind Doug. After her left leg was amputated above the knee, she played the guilt trip card on Doug. Still does today. Lives with her boyfriend who runs a small auto repair shop out of his garage…"

Lainey rubbed her tired and blurry eyes. The clock on her computer showed 1:23 a.m. She closed the file, removed the jump drive and placed it back in the baggie. She wrote a quick email to Mary Chase and asked to meet with her as soon as possible. She stretched her arms above her head and yawned.

"Mary, I still am not sure about any murders being committed, but there are possible motives floating around in my head!"

She turned off her computer, gave Powie a treat, and headed to bed.

Chapter Three

⸎⸎⸎

L ainey pulled into a parking spot directly in front of Babe's House of Caffeine about twenty minutes before Mary Chase had emailed to meet. Sunday afternoons meant the coffee house was usually busy with the after church crowd. The wind had been howling steadily at thirty miles an hour, making the temperature feel below zero. She was thankful she didn't have far to walk to the door.

Babe's had photos of many local celebrities, school groups, and regulars hanging on the walls. Lainey sat at a high-top table that faced the front door and was next to the photo of a local radio announcer raising up a coffee cup. She looked at the black and white photo and read the signed inscription 'Thanks for feeding my coffee cravings!'

A waitress came up to the table. "How's it going?

Our Sunday specials are the firehouse chili or a pound of buffalo wings. What can I get started for you?"

Lainey, putting her iPad on the table and checking her phone said without looking up, "A medium nonfat mocha Frappuccino with no whip cream, please."

She hoped that Mary would be able to answer the many questions she had concerning the data on the jump drive. She looked up to see Mary walking toward her with a purple and yellow Minnesota Vikings stocking cap on her head. Lainey smiled and waved.

Mary, putting her puffy coat on the chair, took off her stocking cap, bent over just a bit to fluff her bright red hair. "I'm so glad you emailed! It means you believe me!" she said, her green eyes sparkling.

"It certainly appears that something may be happening," Lainey replied cautiously, "but I have many questions that were not answered in the files you gave me." She paused as she watched Mary's smile disappear.

"Oh," sighed Mary. Her shoulders slumped forward as she leaned on the table and said in a deadpan voice, "What do you need to know?" She was looking directly into Lainey's eyes as if no one else was in the coffee shop. "I'm not promising to know everything."

Judging by her actions, Lainey knew this meeting might not be as pleasant and friendly as the first one. She paused for a moment before laying her iPad on the table to type.

"I don't mean to cause you to worry or stress, but if there is someone targeting the Sullivan family and your brother, I have questions that must be answered," Lainey said as gently as possible.

Mary nodded. "I understand."

Lainey smiled and looked at her notes for the order of the questions she needed to ask. For years, friends had said she was a perfectionist, that she spent more time organizing notes than a librarian and had laughed stating that Einstein wasn't as anal about notes as she was. She would always smile. It was her personality and how she worked best.

"Who wrote or copied these files onto that jump drive?" Lainey began.

"I got the Sullivan information from the family trees that were connected to us when our DNA results came back. You can get birth dates, marriage records, criminal records, and more when you search for a person through the website," she said, motioning for the waitress to bring her a coffee. "A person could spend days or weeks looking up or searching for lost relatives. I guess you could say it can be addicting. I filled out the GEN file, too."

"You said you got DNA results showing the name Sullivan?" Lainey asked.

In the back of her mind, Lainey was thinking about Della Kristiansen from the Whoopee group. She was obsessed with searching for ancestors. Maybe she could do research on the Sullivans' and Reynolds'.

"The results are posted online and show your DNA matches in order of closeness," Mary sipped her coffee. "Immediate relatives like parents or siblings are listed first, showing the percentage of certainty beside their names. Next, the first or second cousins and so on down to fourth and fifth cousins." She thought for a moment.

"If a person on the match list has set up a family tree and it is public, not only can you look at that one person, but you can see all of their relatives' entries, too. Our family had more than four thousand DNA matches, but only one immediate relative match. The Sullivan tree. That's where we found a birth certificate showing Doug had a different mother than Ann and me."

Lainey caught herself watching Mary's mannerisms instead of intently listening to her. Sitting back in her chair, Mary had been slowly sliding her fingers repeatedly around the top of her coffee cup as she was talking.

Is she nervous? Is she hiding something?

"The paragraph about Doug mentioned he quit school because of an accident?" Lainey questioned.

Mary looked down at the table, fidgeted in her seat, looked up, and said, "Dad died in a tractor accident

Doug's junior year." She wiggled again in the chair and continued.

"Doug was driving our old tractor, doing his regular chores. Dad was working a few feet away, and Ann was standing by the fence watching, drinking a coke. For some reason, the fuel line on the tractor caught fire." Mary stopped and took a long drink of coffee.

"Doug began screaming, trying to fan the flames. Dad ran toward the tractor yelling at him to get off. Doug tried to get down but his boot caught and he was halfway leaning off the side. Dad grabbed Doug, yanked and pulled till he was finally free and pushed him toward the fence," Mary tearfully explained.

"He told Doug to get Ann back to the house as he tried to shovel dirt on the fire. Before Doug could get to Ann, the tractor exploded. Dad was killed instantly. The blast threw Doug to the ground and ruptured his eardrums. When he looked up, Ann was lying on the ground with a huge piece of metal sticking out of her left thigh."

An overwhelming sadness hung over the table that sucked the air from Lainey's lungs.

"Oh my goodness!" Lainey gasped as she put her hand on Mary's. "I am so sorry." For a moment, both were silent. Lainey knew the hurt of losing a parent and could see that Mary had been close to her dad.

"It was many years ago. Farming is a dangerous job." She wiped away a tear with the napkin.

Lainey took a deep breath and continued. "That's when Doug quit school to work the farm. Did your mom work outside the home?"

"No, Mom worked to keep the house running and to take care of Ann."

"Tell me about Ann. What happened to her after the accident?"

Mary's demeanor changed instantly. Lainey sensed anger or frustration and wanted to tread lightly on questions about Ann. She didn't want Mary to stop talking.

"Ann's the baby of the family," she rolled her eyes. "She was born with her left leg much shorter than her right. Dad felt sorry for her and blamed my Mom and her doctor for the defect."

Lainey blinked. "Why did he blame your Mom and her doctor?"

"Mom told me that back in the '60s there was a new wonder drug that was supposed to help morning sickness, dizziness, and insomnia. While she was carrying Ann, she was constantly sick and not able to take care of me or Doug. So, the doctor prescribed this pill for her. When Ann was born, no one thought twice about why she had the birth defect. Sometimes those things happen, I guess," Mary shrugged.

"Several years later, Mom was notified that this wonder drug had been linked to thousands of birth defects in babies born either without arms or legs or with limb defects." She rubbed the right side of her neck and shoulder. "That's when Dad began to blame Mom for Ann's handicap."

A small smirk appeared on Mary's face as she added, "Dad always paid more attention to Ann. He made her wooden canes to use, brought her little presents for no reason. Ann walked with the cane, but never participated in school sports or helped out much on the farm. Dad would do anything for her if she asked. She played up to dad. Anything she did wrong was my fault, or Doug's. Heaven forbid she ever got blamed or was in trouble!" Mary tried to hide the hint of hatred in her voice.

"She wasn't seriously hurt during the accident?" Lainey asked.

"Oh yes, she was. The metal piece that cut into her left leg damaged it so badly that it had to be amputated above the knee. Since Dad wasn't there to baby her, Ann made it her purpose in life to put a guilt trip on Doug. She wanted him to suffer, too." It was obvious Mary was frustrated talking about it.

Her voice grew a bit louder. "Doug felt he caused Dad's death and Ann to lose her leg. Ann became an expert at making Doug feel sorry for her and that it was his place to provide for her."

"Is Ann able to take care of herself?"

"Of course she is!" Mary quickly snapped. "But why should she? Doug pays her house payment, gives her money at her every whim, answers her calls at all hours of the night. It's hard work running a farm by yourself and Doug has done the best he can. He still feels responsible for the accident and has sacrificed everything to make things better for Ann. Doug never married and, in my opinion, will never break free from her grip."

Lainey knew now why none of Mary's children were named Ann. Had the years of anger and resentment pushed her to the breaking point? Was she capable of murder?

"Does Ann live with Doug?" Lainey questioned.

"Ann lives with her boyfriend, Chuck Austin. He runs a small auto repair shop from their garage, Austin's Bang or Bump Shop. Ann doesn't work and spends most of her time playing video games or shopping online...that is, when she is not complaining to Doug about something."

Mary excused herself and went to the restroom to freshen up, giving Lainey a chance to regroup her thoughts and make a few more notes.

Lainey ordered two warm salted pretzels with hot cheddar cheese and a couple of waters.

"Is that everything you need to ask me?" Mary asked as she sat down.

Lainey smiled at the waitress who brought the pretzels and waters.

"Have you got a few more minutes? The Vikings

don't play till 7 p.m. tonight!" Lainey chuckled, hoping that would relax the tension.

Mary grinned. "Feed me and I'll always answer questions!"

"You said the Sullivan family tree was the immediate or close relationship you found when getting Doug's DNA results back. I'm not familiar with these kinds of websites," Lainey confessed. "Are the records or information you found normally listed on public records that anyone can find?"

Mary nodded. "There are birth, death, and marriage records that show they come from public websites from different states and sources. But I think the main reason these sites are important is that they give you names of people to search."

"I did a little research about these types of DNA tests," Lainey began. "It appears that they compare the DNA sample you submit with the ones that have already been submitted from others who use their site or are in their database. So, your DNA is not matched with every single person worldwide."

"That's why we did a couple of DNA tests with different companies," Mary stated. "We thought they might have different members in their system."

"When we met last time you mentioned you have proof from some database law enforcement officials use. What proof? How did you get access to it?" Lainey asked immediately. She was concerned that Mary had somehow broken the law getting access to this information.

"I found a public DNA matching website that allows you to download your results from other testing companies' data bases. It states very plainly that law enforcement has used their information in investigations and that your information might be available to them if you download it," Mary said quickly. "I downloaded Doug's DNA results to see if they also came up with any of the Sullivan's as close relatives."

Lainey studied her face for a moment. "Did Doug know you submitted his information?"

"Not at first, and he was mad when he found out," Mary admitted. "The results from this site were very complicated. It did show the names of the Sullivans, but the results were based on strings of DNA and came in some sort of chart. I'm not a medical person, so trying to decode colors and percentages on separate strings of DNA was overwhelming to me."

Lainey was a bit confused at this point in their conversation. "What makes you think someone has murdered or plans to commit murder? I don't see any evidence in what you have told me or what is on that jump drive. Isn't that the reason you contacted me in the first place?"

Mary's hesitation made Lainey think she had pushed her a bit too far.

"I contacted Raymond Sullivan," she said with a defiant tone. "Doug is killing himself working two jobs trying to make ends meet. I thought if Sullivan knew of him or got to know him, he might offer Doug a job." She finished drinking her water. "I went to his office to see him a few months ago…without Doug's knowledge."

Lainey had to admire her spunk. Showing up at the office of a very successful and probably very busy man like Raymond Sullivan, claiming to be a long lost relative took nerve.

"Did you actually meet him?"

"After a few tries, yes, I did," she explained. "Of course, he didn't believe me and thought I was another person trying to ask for a handout or something." But once I showed him the Sullivan tree and our results, he started to come around."

"What do you mean he started to come around?"

"He had some detective or lawyer or someone on his staff look into my claim that Doug was his older half-brother. Raymond gave me a copy of Doug's original birth certificate that he received from the state. It showed the mother as Stella Baxter and the father as my dad."

"Okay. That proves there is a family connection. But I keep coming back to the question of where the evidence of murder is?"

Mary contemplated her next words carefully before

speaking. "Raymond Sullivan and I are in different social circles and the fact that he agreed to at least meet or talk with Doug surprised me. He asked me, in a polite way, if I was asking him for money or if my family needed financial help. That made me feel sleazy or like some type of moocher," she shivered. "I blurted out that we in no way wanted his crummy money. I explained that I just wanted him to meet Doug and see what a hard worker he was. That's all."

Lainey glanced at her phone to see the time was speeding by. She still needed more proof or something concrete from Mary.

"It's getting late and I need to ask about what the police said when you talked with them."

"After Raymond had the evidence that Doug was his half-brother, I asked him about the recent deaths of his two older brothers, Eugene and Harold. He said that they both died suddenly in freak accidents within a few months of each other."

Lainey nodded. "Yes, I read in your file that Eugene died in a car accident and Harold in a fish house incident."

Mary leaned forward. "Raymond said he thought it was a tragic coincidence at the time but always wondered why no investigations were conducted."

Lainey listened and waited for her to continue.

"Doug is a part-time body driver so I asked him if he could remember being on call for these two death pickups. Turns out he was. He and Chuck Austin transported both bodies."

"Wait… Ann's boyfriend, Chuck?" Lainey asked with her senses tingling.

"Yes, he drives part time, too. I'm no detective or anything, but the two brothers died just after we found out Doug was related to them. I was worried that Raymond might suspect Doug's or my motives to get to know him if he found out Doug had been the body driver," Mary continued. "Since Raymond wondered why no investigation had been done, I thought I would ask Chuck's brother, Nathan, about it. He works as an assistant investigator for the coroner's office."

Lainey's mind was whirling--half-brothers, body drivers, coroner's assistants. This was quickly getting out of her area of expertise.

"This Nathan Austin, could he legally tell you anything?" Lainey asked.

"He said that nothing seemed suspicious and that no further investigations were necessary. Therefore, no autopsies were ordered. I was afraid of doing something illegal, so I took the jump drive and my information to the police station." Mary frowned. "They listened, but said there was no evidence of murder or foul play and could do nothing."

Lainey needed time to think. She was going to need help.

"I have a few friends that might be able to help me.

Would you mind if I share this information with them?"

"I guess so," Mary paused. "Doug is a blood relative of the Sullivans and could possibly inherit some of their fortune. If someone is killing the Sullivans and finds out about Doug, he would be in danger. I'll do whatever I need to do to protect him."

"Great! Thank you, Mary," Lainey said. "I can't promise you anything. Do you mind if I talk with Doug?"

"I thought you might say that." Her voice sounded like someone being scolded. "Let me talk with him first. He thinks this is all nonsense."

The two stood up. "I'll call you in a couple of days, all right?" Lainey asked, giving her a hug.

"Okay," Mary said quietly.

Lainey, watched her leave the coffee shop, sat down, and pulled out her phone. She typed a text to the Whoopee group. "Can we meet tomorrow for supper at my house? Need your help!"

Chapter Four

The aroma of homemade enchiladas and cinnamon sopapillas greeted Francy and Vera as they walked into Lainey's kitchen the next evening.

"Did you make your mom's recipe?" Francy asked as she opened the oven door to inspect the bubbly dish baking inside.

"Sure did. Got your favorite dessert, too!"

Vera laughed and put a small tin filled with assorted chocolate covered nuts and pretzels on the counter.

"I think you are wanting something, my dear."

Lainey smiled and winked. "It's always better to ask for help on a full stomach, isn't it?"

The front door opened and in popped Della with her usual 'Whoop, whoop, whoop.' She sniffed. "Smells yummy! Let's eat!"

After devouring the enchiladas and sopapillas, the ladies quickly cleared the table and Lainey brought out her laptop. Vera put the tin of nuts in the center of the table.

"Thanks for coming over, guys," Lainey began. "I need your help on something and it has to be kept confidential."

Vera, Francy, and Della looked at each other, then back at Lainey. Francy was the first to speak. "This seems serious. What's going on?"

Lainey opened her notes and told them the entire story, including her meetings with Mary Chase. When she finished, Della was the first to speak, shaking her head in disbelief.

"This is bizarre. Seriously? Murdering a family tree of people?"

"I know it sounds crazy." Lainey fixed her gaze on Della. "But Mary believes it."

Francy thought for a moment before speaking. "I remember the police call about the fish house death. I was working that day. The entire department was buzzing about it being Harold Sullivan."

Vera, who had been very quiet, spoke up. "Doc used to treat little Harold. He would tell Doc stories about ice fishing with his dad, catching the big ones. He was such a nice young man."

"Della," Lainey began, "you've done the DNA thing

and gotten matches back. Is Mary right about how matches appear and who can see them?"

"Each website or company has different kinds of reports, but yes, Mary is right. Matches appear based on how closely members already listed in the site's database match your DNA."

"If I understand this, I could be a match to Mary but because I haven't submitted my DNA to this site, the match would not show up. Correct?" Lainey restated to clarify.

"I think that is correct," Della confirmed.

"Are you aware of the website Mary mentioned that law enforcement uses?" Lainey asked.

"There are several sites, and the one she told you is legitimate. Law enforcement can obtain DNA results from anyone who downloads their reports onto that site."

Vera looked a bit startled. "See, I told you! I'm not giving my DNA to anyone! Next thing you know, I'd be a suspect on that television program that looks for criminals or something!"

The ladies laughed.

"Mom, you have no worries. The speeding ticket you got back in the '50s doesn't count anymore!" Francy chuckled.

"It was a warning, not a ticket!" Vera crossed her arms.

Lainey returned her attention to Della. "Would

you check out the Reynolds' family tree online? I want to see if you can find these birth or death records. Maybe you will find something Mary missed."

"I am a member on the same DNA site, and if their tree is public, I should be able to search for it," she answered excitedly.

Suddenly Lainey realized that Francy had been intently studying the iPad notes screen.

"What do you think, Francy?" She asked.

"Mary told you that a guy in the coroner's office said no investigation or autopsy was ordered?"

"That's what she said. A guy named Nathan Austin, who happens to be Mary's sister's boyfriend's brother," Lainey rolled her eyes. "How confusing is that chain of relationships?" She added with a shrug.

"I worked with Ben Sargent for years in the police department," Francy said as if she was thinking out loud. "He's a Corporal now but everyone calls him Sarge. He would know details about both of these deaths. I'm not sure what he would tell us, but I think we need to pay him a visit!"

"I'm in!" Lainey smiled.

"I'll call the station tomorrow and see if he has a little time," Francy said. "Maybe we should meet him for coffee first to feel him out?"

"Sounds great. Let's meet at Babe's if he can."

After the group left, Lainey checked her emails and

noticed one from Mary Chase saying that Doug reluctantly agreed to talk with her.

She quickly replied to the email. It was almost eleven at night and she fought the urge to call Doug right then.

"I guess people do stop working to sleep," she muttered to herself and made a note to call him first thing the next morning.

Lainey woke up early to get a head start on the day, giving herself time to meet with Doug Reynolds if she could. Her morning quickly turned into hectic chaos as she dealt with client emails, phone calls, concerns, and changes in appointment dates. It was almost noon when she finally took a moment to breathe.

"Gosh, everybody needs something, and they want it right now!" She said out loud, raising her arms above her head to stretch.

I have to call Doug!

She pulled up Mary's email and dialed the phone number listed for him. The phone rang for what seemed an eternity before an automated voice message gave the normal spiel that the person you have called is unavailable. Please leave a message. Lainey started to leave a message but heard the voice say that the mailbox was full and to try again later.

"Gee whiz!" she groaned. She dialed again and got the same messages.

Her afternoon was busy, and she was thankful when

the local 6 p.m. news began. She tried calling Doug again. No luck.

Lainey walked into the kitchen, put food down for Powie, and opened the refrigerator. As she stared blankly at the shelves, her phone rang. It was Francy.

"Sarge agreed to meet us," Francy said. "He can meet tomorrow morning on his lunch break about 11:30 or so. Can you make it?"

Lainey checked her calendar. "I will be there! Meeting at Babe's?"

"Yes, unless he gets called away," Francy replied. "He was a bit hesitant, so I'm not sure what, if anything, we might learn from him."

"At least he agreed to meet with us."

"You know cops and free coffee. I might have promised him a sandwich, too," Francy said sheepishly.

"No problem. See you tomorrow!" Lainey chuckled.

The information lifted her spirits. She decided to make herself a spinach, turkey, olive, and goat cheese salad for supper. While she ate, her mind was flooded with questions she needed to ask Sarge. What did he know about the deaths? Did he happen to be on duty when they occurred? Would he get records of the coroner's reports she could see? Had he been the one who spoke with Mary?

She finished her salad, loaded the dishwasher, put four Oreo cookies on a napkin, and took a cold bottle of water out of the refrigerator. "Good thing Oreos make me think better," she laughed to herself and sat on the chair at her desk.

She tried dialing Doug Reynolds once more. This time a man's voice answered. "Yeah," said the man.

Startled, Lainey replied, "Hello! Is this Doug Reynolds?"

"Yeah. Who's this?"

"This is Lainey Maynard. Mary mentioned to you that I was going to call."

"Yeah, she talked to me." There was an awkward pause. "You're wasting your time if you believe her about murders being committed." His voice was filled with frustration or disgust.

"I realize you don't believe Mary's theory," Lainey guardedly continued. "But I told her I would look into it to ease her mind."

"Ease her mind?" He gruffly replied. "Nothing will ease Mary's mind. She needs to drop this idea. No one is killing the Sullivans."

Lainey knew she had to tread lightly here or lose any chance of meeting with him. "I know you are very busy, but would you have a minute to meet with me? I'll come to the farm if that is more convenient for you."

Again he paused. Too long of a pause, Lainey thought. She added, "There are a couple of questions I have and only you have the answers to them. Would you please meet with me?"

She could hear him sigh before he answered. "All right. Be at the farm by 7 a.m. in the morning. I can talk to you then."

"Thank you! I'll be there!"

She put it in her calendar.

Meeting with Doug early, then with Sarge at 11:30. Tomorrow should be an interesting day!

She sent an email to her work that she'd be taking a vacation day tomorrow and went to bed with a thousand thoughts running through her mind. By 3:30 a.m. the next morning, Lainey was up, dressed, and organizing her questions for Doug.

As she drove to his farm, she turned the radio to classic bluegrass music and was singing along, sipping her usual morning mocha Frappuccino.

The entrance to the farm had a tall, arched sign with the Reynolds' name proudly displayed. It reminded her of an old western movie set. It was weather worn. She drove over the cattle guard and under the arch to follow the dirt road to the house.

Lainey knocked on the screen door and waited for Doug to answer.

"Come on in, it's open."

She opened the door. Inside the smell of bacon and fresh bread made her stomach growl. She could see down the narrow hallway into the kitchen where Doug was standing at the sink.

He looked at Lainey. "Make yourself at home. Breakfast is waiting."

She sat down at the small wooden table that was filled with plates of scrambled eggs, bacon, and fresh biscuits with gravy.

"Oh, my!" Lainey tried not to sound so elated to see the food. "You didn't have to make breakfast for me! It smells delicious."

"Was making breakfast for myself anyway, no trouble to make enough for two," Doug said as he poured two glasses of water. "You can eat and talk at the same time, right?" he added, smiling.

Lainey chuckled. "You bet!"

Sure enough, breakfast tasted as good as it smelled.

"Thank you for meeting with me. I know you must have a lot of work to do."

He nodded. "What's your question."

Not wanting to waste much time, Lainey cut to the chase.

"Have you met with Raymond Sullivan or any of the Sullivan brothers?"

He straightened his shoulders. "Mary tell you that? Yeah, I met with Harold first, then Raymond, but I didn't ask them for money if that's what you're getting at."

"No, I didn't think that," she answered quickly. "What was their reaction to the news that you were the older half-brother?"

"I didn't believe these DNA results at first and neither did they. It was several weeks before any of us started to realize it was true." He finished his water, setting the glass on the table. "Mary wasn't the one who pushed me into meeting them. It was Ann's idea."

Lainey was surprised. "Ann's idea?"

"She went to their office first, showed them the proof, and asked them to meet with me. I wasn't a bit pleased about her going there, and I told her so."

Lainey's mind was spinning. She spoke before she thought. "How did Ann get to the cities and their office? Does she drive?"

She could see Doug tense up with the question about Ann.

"No, Chuck drove her down."

"Chuck Austin, her boyfriend?"

"Yeah."

Lainey was afraid to ask more questions about Ann. She needed to talk with Ann first hand.

"Meeting two unknown half-brothers must have been awkward," she said, hoping to change the subject away from Ann.

"It sure was. But in the end, they seemed to be nice guys."

"Were you in touch with them after that meeting?"

"We are not going to be close buddies," he started, "but we did talk a couple of times on the phone and agreed to meet occasionally or at holidays."

Doug stood up to carry dishes to the sink. Lainey knew her time with him was limited.

"When Eugene and Harold died suddenly, I called to give my condolences, and haven't spoken to Raymond since then," he offered.

"Mary mentioned you had a part-time job as a body driver and that she was hoping you might be able to drive for one of Sullivan's turkey plant operations sometimes."

"Yeah, she thought I was going to ask for a job. I work hard and I wasn't about to ask for a handout just because I was suddenly related to them," he said defiantly. "That's not who I am."

Lainey stood and began walking to the front door. "I understand. Thank you, Doug. I'll let you get to work. If I have any more questions, can I call you?"

"You can call, but I don't usually answer till I'm through for the day. The best time to catch me is after 9 p.m."

"Will do!" Lainey shook his hand. "Thank you for a terrific breakfast and for talking with me. You take care!"

He nodded. "You're welcome."

As Lainey got back into her car, Doug was already out the door, walking toward one of the three red barns beside the house.

He's a hard worker...and a really good cook. She smiled.

Lainey stopped by her home and checked in with

her work before getting ready to meet with Sarge and Francy at 11:30 a.m.

She had a long list of questions for Sarge.

I hope he will know these answers.

As usual, Lainey arrived about fifteen minutes early, got a table, and waited for Francy and Ben Sargent.

To her surprise, a tall, stocky-built officer opened the door and headed directly to her table.

She stood up and put out her hand to greet him. "Hello, Officer Sargent."

"Hello, Ms. Maynard," the officer said as he shook her hand with a grip that could have easily crushed a bone.

"How did you know to come to this table? Have we met before?" She asked as they sat down.

"No, Ma'am," Sarge replied. "Francy showed me your picture."

Lainey nodded. Good old Francy. "She should be here any time." Sarge smiled and nodded.

As if on cue, Francy raced in the door talking a mile a minute.

"Sorry if I'm late! Had to stop and put gas in the car! Seems it won't go without it!"

"No worries," Lainey said. "Let's order and talk while we wait. Okay?"

Francy ordered her favorite bacon and peanut butter hamburger with fries and Lainey, still full of breakfast, ordered the lite tuna and kale salad.

"I'll have the grilled walleye sandwich with horseradish and an extra side of red sauce. No fries," Sarge said without looking at the menu.

He must come here often.

"May I call you Sarge?" Lainey asked.

"Everyone calls me Sarge," he smiled. "Francy mentioned you were an insurance investigator. What can I help you with?"

She began, "I'm not here with my job, officially, but a bit of personal investigation, if you will."

Francy frowned a bit. "Mary Chase asked Lainey to look into her idea that someone or some persons might be murdering relatives," she said to hasten up the conversation. She glanced at Lainey.

"Mary Chase?" Sarge asked. "Mary Reynolds Chase?"

Lainey had a surprised look on her face. "Yes! Were you the officer she spoke with a couple of weeks ago?"

"I did speak with Mary," Sarge was hesitant with his reply.

Lainey thought it might be difficult getting information from him. She had texted Mary earlier that morning asking her to give permission for Sarge to share information about their meeting.

"I have a text message from Mary this morning giving you permission to talk with us about your meeting. We can call her now if you need to." She showed him the message. "Can I ask you about the meeting?"

Sarge read the message, took in a deep breath and said, "Why are you interested in my meeting with Mary?"

Francy piped in. "Mary asked Lainey to help her get proof that someone is murdering the Sullivans."

Lainey sighed. Leave it to Francy to get straight to the point.

"Yes, Mary still believes that Eugene and Harold were murdered, and that Raymond Sullivan and her brother Doug are in danger."

Lainey realized that her cards were on the table before she had even had a chance to get a good feeling about Sarge. She didn't like showing her hand so early.

"I see. Mary did explain to me about the DNA results showing her brother as a half-brother to the Sullivans. She had information on her computer that she'd brought with her." Lainey thought his answer sounded very rehearsed and way too business-like.

"Her concern about the deaths of Eugene and Harold Sullivan was founded only by hearsay, and perhaps speculation on her part," Sarge began. "I assured her that learning about unknown relatives through DNA public testing sites or the coincidence of two deaths in that new family line was not considered evidence that would point to an act of murder."

Francy cut her eyes over to Lainey as if to say I told you so.

Lainey nodded slightly. "I understand that. However, Mary said that no autopsy was ordered on either body. Why? What dictates whether one is ordered or not?" She was trying to look tough and inquisitive at the same time.

Sarge's response sounded like a memorized script.

"The coroner's office is called to the scene of any reported death. The coroner or medical examiner may order an autopsy, at the coroner or medical examiner's sole discretion. In the case of any human death when in the judgment of the coroner or medical examiner, the public interest would be served by an autopsy."

He looked into Lainey's eyes and she felt he was trying to see how much she comprehended. Her eyes narrowed and she had to guard herself against the blatant insult she felt.

"I didn't realize the coroner had the power to decide that."

"There are many circumstances that do require an autopsy be ordered. But the two deaths Mary is concerned with were ruled accidental and the coroner ordered no autopsy for either."

Sensing tension in Lainey, Sarge added, "I apologize if you felt I was reciting from a textbook to you, Ms. Maynard. That was not my intent."

"Thank you." She glanced at Francy who was looking down at her hands.

"Was there a police report filed for each death?" Lainey asked.

"Yes."

"May I have a copy of those reports?"

"No," Sarge replied. "Only the family can get copies of police reports."

"I see." She thought for a moment and continued. "How did Mary know that autopsies were not ordered?"

"She did not give me that information. She had no copies of any official documents of any kind."

Lainey's mind began racing. *Documents? Would there be additional reports of the accidents?*

Sarge looked at his watch. "I need to be going. Thank you for lunch. If you have any questions, let me know."

Francy hugged him and Lainey shook his hand.

"Thank you, Sarge. I think we will be seeing more of each other." Lainey's smile was genuine.

"Francy has the office number. Leave a message and I will get back with you. Have a good day."

After Sarge left, Francy looked at Lainey.

"Okay. Something is going on in your brain. What is it?"

"Did you hear him say documents? That means

there are other reports somewhere." She looked at Francy and grinned like a hungry bobcat.

"Do you still have access to files at the police station?" She asked as she put her hand on Francy's shoulder.

"I know that look," her friend said hesitantly, sitting back in the chair. "And it has trouble written all over it!"

Lainey smiled. "Can you get access to files at the station or not, silly."

"They call me to fill in when they are short-handed. Let me see if they need me anytime soon." She pulled out her cell phone to call. "If they do, maybe I can look around if no one is in the station during my shift."

"Or I can come to visit you and do the snooping around!" Lainey said slyly.

Chapter Five

✤✤✤

The next morning, Francy called Lainey to say that she was going to fill in on the graveyard shift that same evening. Lainey's heart raced with excitement.

"Great!" she almost screamed into the phone. "What time should I come?"

"You have to be careful. At night, the station is very quiet, but I never know when an officer will bring in a prisoner, or when someone is going to show up in the office. The shift is from 7 p.m. to 7 a.m. Let's plan on 11:30 p.m. or so. I'll call you and let you know it's safe."

"Thanks, Francy. I'll be careful, I promise! See you tonight."

Lainey's thoughts turned to Ann. Why had she been the one to make first contact with the Sullivans? What did the Sullivans think of her? How disabled was she?

She decided to contact Raymond Sullivan's office on the chance he might have a minute to meet with her. She dialed the office and a young woman answered politely, yet business-like.

"Sullivan's Best Poultry. This is Margo. How may I help you?"

"Hello." Knowing she didn't have long to make her point before the woman cut her off, she continued, "I'm Lainey Maynard, an insurance investigator, and I was hoping to meet with Raymond Sullivan briefly today, if possible."

"What is the nature of your visit with him?" Margo asked. "Mr. Sullivan has a very busy schedule."

"I realize he is very busy, and I would only need a few moments of his time." Lainey hoped her reply would satisfy Margo's questions.

"If this is a legal matter, Mr. Sullivan will request you speak to his attorney." Margo's voice was monotone. "I will need to know the nature of your business before I can give you the attorney's office information."

Thinking quickly, Lainey responded, "I am not at liberty to share the reasons for my meeting with anyone other than Mr. Sullivan. Would he happen to have a couple of minutes to fit me in between his scheduled appointments? It is extremely important that I speak with him at his earliest convenience." She hoped her voice hadn't been too demanding.

Margo was very curt with her reply. "Mr. Sullivan is not in at the moment. Please leave your phone number and I will check with him when he returns."

Lainey knew the woman was brushing her off, but she recited her phone number anyway. She also decided it was time to go to Sullivan's office and sit until she *could* speak with him. She thanked Margo and headed to her bedroom to change her clothes.

Her favorite outfit to wear when presenting a case or meeting with a high-powered client was a pair of solid black legging-type slacks, a black knit blouse or mock turtleneck and either her blood red Western style blazer with shiny sparkles in the fabric or her deep purple and grey leather Southwestern blazer. Lainey loved dark, bright colors and the blazers gave her a feeling of power, strength, and control. In her mind, it was an advantage.

The office of Sullivan's Best Poultry was more than an hour from Mirror Falls and Lainey was on the road before eleven that morning. She was determined to sit in the office until Margo allowed her to see Mr. Sullivan. She had her iPad and phone to keep up with work.

As she drove into the tiny parking garage, she thought how beautiful the Stone Arch Bridge area was and wondered what it would be like to have an office overlooking the river. She gathered her thoughts, her coffee mug, and iPad and walked inside to wait for the elevator. When the door opened, she punched the top floor button and stepped back.

When she reached the top floor and the door finally opened, Lainey was startled to see Raymond Sullivan standing there, ready to get on, looking at her. Their eyes met briefly as she stepped out of the elevator.

"Hello, Mr. Sullivan. I'm Lainey Maynard and I called your office to meet with you today."

Raymond's eyes narrowed a bit as he looked at her coffee mug and iPad. Without changing expressions he said, "If you are going to pour that coffee on me, forget it. I'm not going to the dry cleaners today."

Lainey couldn't tell if he was joking or serious. She smiled. "No sir, my intent was not to spill coffee on you today. I try only to spill on your regular laundry days." She hoped that would lighten his mood.

Raymond smiled slightly. "Excuse me, I have an appointment," he said pushing the down button on the elevator.

Lainey saw an opening. "Please, Mr. Sullivan, I am Lainey Maynard and…"

Raymond interrupted her mid-sentence and said, "Yes, I did hear you say that."

Okay, she thought, if you want to play that way, here goes.

"I need to speak with you about Doug Reynolds."

Raymond hesitated. "Who are you?" He asked without taking his eyes off the elevator door.

"I am here on a request from Doug's sister, Mary Chase. She is concerned for your safety and her brother's. Can we please talk for a few minutes? Please."

His gaze left the elevator and found Lainey's eyes as if he were probing to read her mind. The elevator door opened. Raymond continued to focus on Lainey and the door shut again.

"If you will throw the coffee cup away, I have five minutes to talk with you." He sighed as he headed back to his office.

She nodded and followed. As Raymond opened the office door, Margo looked up with surprise.

"Mr. Sullivan! Did you forget something?"

Lainey looked at the young woman. She had beautiful amber hair that was put up neatly in a bun and she was wearing a gorgeous blue couture designed dress that fit her like a glove. She was not smiling as she looked at Lainey.

"Everything is fine, Margo," Raymond answered. "This is Lainey Maynard. Please reschedule my afternoon appointment for this evening."

"Yes, sir," Margo said with a strange look her face. "Will you be long?"

"Not long. Please hold my calls," he answered as he walked into his office. He looked at Lainey, her coffee cup, and motioned for her to come in. "Please, sit down."

Lainey nodded and looking around briefly, sat her coffee cup on Margo's neatly organized desk, shrugged and said, "Sorry! Don't see a trash can!" She smiled and hurried into Raymond's office.

The office was exactly like the picture Lainey had seen on the jump drive. She marveled at the view from the windows. "I admire this view! I bet it is easy to daydream looking through the windows, isn't it?"

For the first time, she saw a little smile on Raymond's face. "Yes, it can be mesmerizing." He looked at her and said, "If I may call you Lainey, I really do not have much time. What can I help you with?"

"Please, let me say first I am sorry for the recent loss of your brothers. That must be difficult for you."

"Thank you. Yes, losing them both has been difficult to accept."

"Mary Chase spoke with me about her concerns that your brothers' deaths were not accidental. She fears that both you and Doug are in danger." She watched for his reaction.

"Do you know the circumstances around discovering the relationship between Doug Reynolds and my family?" He asked curiously.

"Yes, Mary told me the story of how their DNA search showed that Doug's mother was your mother. I have also spoken with him. Mary did speak with you about her thoughts about murder?" She asked hesitantly.

Raymond leaned forward, resting his elbows on the chair's armrests. "I did speak with Mary. I realize she believes that my brothers were murdered. However, I do not share those feelings." He appeared to be looking for a response from Lainey and when none came, he continued.

"The discovery of an older brother was new to everyone, and I admire Mary's concern for our wellbeing. But the police have assured me that my brothers were involved in unfortunate accidents."

"It does seem a bit of a stretch to think that your brothers were murdered, but it is a strange coincidence that the accidents happened so very close to each other. As an investigator, I have to consider all possibilities until they are proven false. And Mary did ask me to look into this for her peace of mind. I hope you understand."

"Of course. Doug appears to be a good man and if answering your questions will help, then by all means ask away."

"Thank you." Lainey pulled out her iPad to take notes. "Do you have a copy of the police reports from the accidents?"

"No. The police explained to me what happened and that there was nothing suspicious about either accident that would warrant further investigation. I admit the accident with Harold happening so close to Eugene's made me wonder for a moment, but law enforcement officials are the professionals who investigate these incidents, so I believe their findings."

"Now that you are aware that Doug is your half-brother, would he stand to inherit any of the Sullivan estate?" She wondered if that question was too personal.

Raymond had a look of surprise on his face. She could see he was debating on what to say before speaking aloud. "Families who have some degree of wealth often deal with the question of who their rightful heir is, especially after the death of prominent community family members. We have an army of attorneys who have protected the Sullivan name and business for years. Several are personal friends and are my first line of defense."

Raymond leaned back in his chair. "When Doug's birth certificate was proven to be legitimate and that he was an older half-brother, my attorneys became involved immediately. I met with him a few times with the attorneys present. Doug insisted that he was not interested in inheriting anything from the Sullivan estate. His sister, Ann, came to me to ask for a job for him. When I spoke with Doug about possibly working part time or if he needed financial help, he was insulted and said vehemently that he did not want anything other than friendship from me. I did not mention it again."

Interesting. The subject of Ann again...how does she fit in?

Raymond looked at the crystal clock on his desk. "I need to be going. Is that everything?"

"Yes." Lainey smiled, shut, her iPad, and stood. "You have been a huge help. If I do have more questions or if I do find indications that perhaps the accidents were something more involved, may I speak with you again?" She offered her hand.

"Of course. It would be best if you contact me via my personal email." He took a business card off his desk, wrote his email on the back and handed it to Lainey. "I will answer when I can."

Lainey thanked him and turned to leave.

"By the way, if we plan to meet again, my dry cleaning is done on Thursdays. They specialize in coffee stains," he said with an elfish grin.

Lainey smirked, not knowing if he was being funny or sarcastic. "I'll try to remember that."

She walked past Margo's desk and reached for the door when she heard her name called. She turned around to see Margo standing in front of her holding the coffee cup she had left on her desk earlier.

"You forgot this." Margo pushed the cup into Lainey's hand. "There is a garbage container in the parking garage."

Lainey smiled and held her tongue while she watched Margo go back to her desk.

"Hope she has the same dry cleaner as Raymond," Lainey said under her breath as she went out the door.

Turning on I-94 to head back to Mirror Falls, she noticed a missed call from Francy. She turned on her Bluetooth and waited for her friend to answer.

"Hey, Lainey."

"Hey, Francy. Sorry I missed your call. What's up?"

"I was thinking about tonight and what if you brought Mom with you?"

"Vera? Why?"

"Mom used to stop in unexpectedly and bring treats to the department during my shift. Everyone loves my mom and wouldn't think anything was out of the ordinary if she came while I'm working," she explained. "What do you think?"

"Sounds like a plan. Will you ask her?"

"I mentioned it to her earlier. She's ready and willing!" Francy laughed.

"Your mom and treats creating a distraction while I snoop around. Who would have thought it!" Lainey chuckled. "Tell her I'll pick up her at eleven."

Vera was looking out the front door waiting anxiously when Lainey pulled into the driveway. Before she could get out of the car, Vera had locked the front door and was walking towards her with two plastic containers of goodies. Lainey had to smile.

"Got everything, Vera?" Lainey asked.

"I'm armed with my favorite cocoa striped cookies,

ginger bars, and homemade mini donuts," she said proudly. "And, I have enough to feed an army!"

"Great!" Lainey laughed. "But let's hope an army of people don't show up tonight!"

"They won't leave hungry if they do!" Vera chuckled. "I'll keep everyone busy!"

Lainey was a little worried as she rang the outside door buzzer at the police department. She needed to see the police report and hoped that she and Vera could get in and out quickly without anyone seeing them. She heard Francy's voice over the intercom. "Give me a second and I'll open the door."

There was a click and soon Lainey and Vera were inside the building facing a half-wall of window openings. Behind the middle one sat Francy.

"I'll buzz you in." She said as the door buzzed open.

Lainey held the door for Vera and her goodies. The purple light on Francy's headset was on, suggesting she was live with someone on the phone or radio. Quietly, they walked over to her desk and waited.

"10-4," Francy said as she clicked off the headset. She stood to give them a hug. "It's been a busy night so far and you will have to be very careful as people are coming and going."

Lainey shook her head as Vera put down the treats and took off her coat. She was dressed in a black turtleneck, black slacks, solid black shoes and socks and she didn't take off her black gloves or her black stocking cap.

"Why are you dressed like that?" Francy asked looking at her oddly. "You hate wearing black!"

"Well….cat burglars in the movies always wear black so they can't be seen and don't leave fingerprints. If it works for them, it should work for us!" Vera said confidently.

Lainey looked at Francy and both burst out laughing. Noticing that Vera was looking a bit hurt, Lainey smiled and said, "We are not cat burglars and we aren't stealing anything."

"You never know. I was just trying to protect us, that's all!" She smiled as she took off her gloves.

Francy rolled her eyes. "I came in early and was able to find out that the filing clerk is far behind. Her desk might be a good place to start looking," she directed.

"Where is her desk or office?" Lainey asked looking around.

"The clerk's office is down the hall, second door on the right. Her office is next to Sarge's office. He comes and goes through the back door, which means he will walk past the clerk's office to get to his. Be careful. He's been in twice this shift already."

Lainey nodded.

Vera asked, "Want me to stand by the backdoor and be the lookout?"

"Mom, if you stand by the back door, anyone

coming in will know something is up! The guys would expect you to be up here with me or waiting for me in the break room."

"I guess you're right," Vera answered disappointedly.

Francy spoke, almost as if giving orders, "Mom, sit in the chair behind me for now. We can take the treats to the break room in a minute. Lainey, normally if the clerk is behind in filing, she has several baskets on her desk either labeled with dates or case numbers. Look at those first. I think the filing cabinets are locked." Francy stated.

"Will do. How will I know if someone is coming, either front or back door?" she asked.

"The hall echoes a good deal. If I buzz the door open for someone, you will hear the loud clicking sound and our voices. If someone is coming in the back door, you will hear the door pushed open and shut. You won't have much time to turn off lights and try to hide under the desk. If that happens, stay under the desk and I'll come to get you when the coast is clear."

Lainey again nodded that she understood. As she walked down the hallway Francy added, "Seriously, don't dilly dally. I'll be in trouble if you're caught."

We'll all be in deep trouble if I'm caught. Lainey stood in front of the clerk's office. Her heart was racing a bit when she flipped on the light.

The small room had grey, metal filing cabinets set

up in a U-shape that took up more than half of the room. The cabinets surrounded an old metal desk with a black rubber finish on the top. Manila files were in piles across the front of the desk with yellow and green sticky notes stuck to the top of each pile. There were three wire baskets that held more manila files with more sticky notes. Smack dab in the middle of the desk sat a large computer screen. Pens, pencils, erasers, candy wrappers, and more papers haphazardly littered the desk. In the right hand corner was one picture of a family of four, dressed in what looked like their Sunday best.

"That reminds me of the Easter pictures my mom used to take." Lainey said softly.

She began looking at each pile on the desk. The first stack looked to have thirty manila files and each had a name and a number on the file's tab. Lainey ran her fingers through the folders and said out loud, "Smith 2385, Fre 4332, Hut 0964. These must be the last name and file number."

No tabs on the next two stacks of files had anything resembling the name Sullivan, Eugene, or Harold either.

Lainey looked through the rest of the piles on the desk. She was starting to worry that she would find nothing. Suddenly she heard a loud squeaky sound and then a door shut. Her heart jumped into her throat as she lunged at the light switch. She threw herself under the small desk, praying whoever it was would walk past.

She heard footsteps that seemed to pause at the clerk's door before moving forward. Her head was pounding, and her chest felt like someone was hitting it with a sledge hammer with each heartbeat.

Lainey tried to control her breathing and to keep from panicking. She listened as she heard familiar voices.

"Hello, Vera," Ben Sargent greeted. "I see we pulled Francy back from retirement."

"Why hello, Sarge!" Vera said without hesitation. "You look the same as you did years ago!" She added, giving him a hug.

"Mom brought treats for the department like the old days," Lainey heard Francy say.

"They are in the break room waiting for you," Vera put her hand on Sarge's arm.

"I'll grab one or two on my way out," Sarge told her. His voice lowered and Lainey could hear a conversation between Francy and Sarge but couldn't make out any words. She was crouched under the desk opening, arms grasping her knees close to her chest.

Poop! Leave quickly, Sarge!

After what seemed like hours, Lainey heard Sarge say, "That's it for now Francy. I'm on call if something comes up."

"You bet, Sarge."

Lainey heard footsteps coming toward her which made her heart beat even harder. Then she heard Sarge say, "By the way, that's not your Mom's vehicle in the parking lot." For a second, Lainey couldn't catch her breath.

"Oh, she borrowed a neighbor's. Her car is in the shop." Lainey hoped Francy's explanation was good enough to satisfy Sarge.

"Okay. I'm going home." Sarge continued down the hallway and out the back door.

Lainey was frozen, not wanting to get out too quickly in case he returned or forgot something.

She heard very fast footsteps and Francy's voice. "Where are you?"

Lainey slowly untwisted her arms and legs and crawled out from under the desk. "I was under the desk!" she said as Francy bolted through the door.

"Holy Smokes that was close!" She said helping Lainey to her feet. "Did you find anything?"

Lainey stretched to her full height and arched her back, raising her arms over her head. "Not yet. None of the files on her desk say anything about the Sullivan brothers. Where else would they be?"

Francy shrugged. "Try the baskets on top of each filing cabinet. When I filed, I would put folders in alphabetical order on top of the drawer they were to go in."

Lainey agreed. Francy's headset lit up once again.

"Gotta go. Please hurry up!"

Lainey looked for the filing cabinet with the letter S on the label. It was the seventh cabinet and had four drawers. She quickly tried to open the filing cabinet. It was locked. She pulled the three wire baskets that sat on top of the cabinet closer so she could look through them.

"Hot dog!" Lainey said loudly enough that Vera and Francy heard her. She pulled out two manila folders that were named E. Sullivan and H. Sullivan. "I found them!"

Lainey heard more footsteps and Vera, almost shouting said, "Don't touch anything! I'm bringing my gloves!"

Francy followed Vera into the clerk's office. "Did you find the police reports?"

Opening the E. Sullivan file and looking through the papers quickly, Lainey replied, "Yes, it's here!" She pulled out her phone camera from her pocket and took pictures of the police reports and other documents in the two Sullivan files.

Francy was pacing back and forth and obviously concerned about how much time this was taking.

"Lainey, you have to go. I've sent two squad cars out and they will be bringing prisoners in very soon."

"Okay, okay." Lainey reluctantly put back the papers, returned the files to their correct wire basket, and quickly left the clerk's office. "I'll go home and look through them."

"Great. I'm here till 7 a.m. I hope you found everything because I'm not cut out for this spying stuff. My blood pressure is through the roof!" Francy declared.

Vera put on her coat and Lainey hugged Francy.

"Thank you, Francy! I could not have gotten this without your help. You are the best!"

"Yea, yea. That's what everyone says." She buzzed the door to let them out.

"And what about the old Mom and her treats? I never get credit!" Vera threw her arms up in the air and shook her head.

They all chuckled before Francy strongly suggested Lainey get her cat burglar mom home.

"Thank you again. I'll see she gets in safely."

"Call me when you get home," Francy said. "I want to know what you found."

"Will do."

Lainey dropped off Vera and made sure she was inside the house before leaving the driveway. Finally, she could take a deep breath without her heart bursting. She wanted, no needed, a mocha frappe - and just this once, she wanted a large... with whole milk and extra whipped cream!

Chapter Six

Lainey hurried into her house, sat her coffee on the kitchen counter, and pulled out her cell phone.

"It's 1:30 a.m.," she said to her cat who was purring loudly. "Ready for a long night, Powie?"

She took her reading glasses from her fanny pack and opened the photos on her phone. The pictures had a brown tint and a couple were blurry. "I must have been shaking more than I thought!" she said. "Think I'll print these out and enlarge them."

Soon the selected photos were sent to her wireless printer. By the time she walked from the kitchen to her office, the printer was spitting out the pages onto the floor. The printer's sliding paper catcher had long since been broken because Powie had decided to take a nap on it.

She picked up the papers, went back to the kitchen counter, took a big gulp of coffee, and started reading. The next time she looked up, her phone clock read 3:16 a.m.

Lainey looked over the notes she'd written on her iPad. Chilling thoughts were cluttering her mind and suddenly she had goose bumps all over. She was beginning to believe Mary Chase. Someone murdered the Sullivans. And she had a gut feeling she knew who.

She called Francy at the police station." I need to talk with Sarge. I'm going to see Ann Reynolds today."

The tone of Lainey's voice and the business-like way she spoke told Francy there was trouble.

"You found evidence?" Francy said quietly. "We have a full house in the office, and I can't talk. Want me to call Sarge now?"

Lainey paused to think. "Could he meet with me this evening? I have to speak with Ann first."

"I'll email him before I leave. Want me to come when you visit Ann?"

"You get some sleep. I'll fill you in when I know something positive."

"You got it. I'll ask Sarge to email or call you with a time. Be careful."

"Sounds good. Talk with you later." Lainey pushed the end call button on the phone, yawned, and looked at Powie who had been sleeping in the chair next to her. "I need a nap to clear my mind. Let's hit the sack."

For a couple of hours, Lainey tossed and turned, trying to force herself to sleep. Finally she gave up, got up, and turned on the news. She was showered and dressed before 7 a.m.

"There's a lot to do today," she said to Powie, running her hand down his back. "I hope Ann likes surprise visitors because I'm going to see her."

Lainey took a neon green sticky note and listed three things. 1. Call Della. 2. Drive to Ann's. 3. Sarge. She stuck the note to the back of her phone.

She waited till about 8 a.m. to call Della, who was not a morning person. Lainey phoned her anyway, knowing she was more than likely sleeping.

"Sorry, it's early Della, but I need to talk with you. Can I come over?"

"Now? You want to come over now? What's wrong?" Della's muttering became coherent words almost immediately.

"I'll explain when I get there. See you in a few minutes."

Mirror Falls was a small town and even though Della technically lived across town, it was only a few minutes' drive, even during rush hour. Lainey checked her emails first and noticed one from Sarge saying he could meet at his office around eight that night. She saved the time to her phone calendar and headed to Della's.

Lainey rang the doorbell and Della answered, still

wearing her night clothes—a satin, zebra-striped pajama robe and her fluffy sheepskin house shoes.

"Girl, what in the world is going on?" she asked as Lainey followed her into the living room.

"I have more information about Mary Chase's ideas that the Sullivan family is being murdered, and I need to ask you a favor."

"You know I'll help you with anything I can." Della gave her a big hug. "Is this about the DNA family tree you wanted me to research?"

"Yes, and no. Did you find out anything else when you looked through the Sullivan and Reynolds family trees on the website?"

"No. Everything Mary had written down was listed on the two family trees," Della answered. "Other than perhaps a few third or fourth generation cousins, I found nothing."

"I thought so, but thank you for checking."

Della had a cinnamon coffee cake on the counter, and she cut a slice for Lainey and herself. "Want some coffee or juice?"

"I'm full of caffeine, but ice water sounds great." She waited for Della to pour the water and sit down before she reluctantly continued.

"I need to ask you a favor and I'm not sure your hubby can know about it."

Della looked very surprised and a bit speechless. "In Heaven's name, what it is?"

"Last night I got the police reports for the accidental deaths of Eugene and Harold Sullivan and I think there is evidence that they were murdered."

Della's mouth dropped open and her eyes widened. She swallowed hard and repeated the word "Murdered?"

Lainey nodded. "The report shows that both bodies were taken to Paul's funeral home."

"I see," Della said slowly. "Why is that an issue?"

"I'm not sure, but I need to look through Paul's records. There wasn't an autopsy ordered for either man, so these records might shed light as to why."

"Why not ask him?"

"I wasn't hired officially to investigate these deaths and I'm not sure Paul could show me the records," Lainey admitted.

"So, we need to sneak in and take a peek, is that what you're saying?"

Lainey half-shrugged and sighed. "In a nutshell, yes."

Della sat back and put her hand to her chin to think. "There's more you are not telling me. Spill it!"

"This is a working theory and I plan on meeting with Francy's officer friend this evening. The police reports show that the bodies were taken to Kristiansen's Funeral Home and the body drivers were Doug Reynolds and Chuck Austin."

Della looked startled. "Doug Reynolds? The brother of Mary Chase?"

"Yes, and Chuck Austin turns out to be Ann Reynolds' live in boyfriend."

Della raised her eyebrows. "Okay, I'm officially curious and intrigued. What else?"

Lainey pulled out her iPad notes. "The investigator from the coroner's office was named Nathan Austin. Coincidence?"

"And you think this Chuck and Nathan are relatives?" Della asked.

"That's a good question. Can we look at those DNA sites and maybe find out?"

"Let's go see!" They walked into the den where her computer was already turned on.

Della logged onto her favorite ancestral research site. She typed the name Chuck Austin. "It's a long shot, Lainey, since we don't have a birth date or middle name."

"I'm going to Ann's house when I leave here. If you can't find anything now, I'll ask her about it."

The search results showed pages and pages of possible entries. "This would take forever Lainey. Let's try again after you speak with Ann."

"I agree. When can we get into Paul's records without him knowing?"

"Hmm…It would have to be after hours so no employees are around. Let me talk with him to see what the schedule of viewing or funerals are for the next couple of days."

"I really need to look today. I'm trying to get evidence to show Sarge when I meet with him this evening."

Della pursed her lips and blew out a whistle. "Well, that's going to be difficult. Let me do some thinking."

"I appreciate it. I'll call you once I leave Ann's house. I'm heading over there now."

"Does she know you are coming?"

"Nope." Lainey winked, picked up her iPad, and walked to the door. "It's a surprise!"

It was a typically cloudy and cold morning, and Lainey was rehearsing what to say when she arrived at Ann's house. Her GPS was leading her North of town to a remote, wooded area where many locals had cabins.

She saw what looked like a metal windmill base that had a sign on the top instead of the round windmill blades. The sign read Austin's Bump or Bang Shop with an arrow pointing to the right. She turned onto a long, unpaved driveway that led to a small log cabin. Beside the cabin was a large metal building with another sign for the repair shop. There were a bunch of cars parked all around the house and garage.

Lainey found a spot close to the cabin to park.

Breathe deep, Lainey, and don't take no for an answer!

She walked toward the front door and knocked

several times. She could hear a female voice inside say, "Just a minute." The door finally opened.

"Are you here to pick up a car?" the woman asked. She was not as tall as Lainey and was on the heavier side. Her hair was about chin length on one side and cut very close to her head on the other side. The longer side had purple streaks in the front.

"Hello, my name is Lainey Maynard and I was hoping to speak with Ann Reynolds."

"I don't know you," the woman replied as she started to close the door.

Lainey stuck her hand on the door and said quickly, "I know your sister, Mary. Can I talk with you for a minute?"

The woman opened the door again. She did not look amused. "Why?" she said bluntly.

"It's about Doug and the Sullivans," Lainey replied just as bluntly. She could see Ann's eyes narrowing. There was no emotion or smile on her face.

Ann opened the door wider and motioned for her to come in. Lainey took a breath and walked into the house. She watched Ann, who walked with a limp, make her way to the couch and sit down. There was no cane in sight.

The cabin wasn't neat, but it wasn't a mess either. The wooden furniture looked newer and had green plaid coverings. Pillows shaped like bears were at either end. Lainey glanced into one of the bedrooms to see two large computer screens, an expensive looking padded desk chair and a futurist desk lamp that was shaped like a figure 8.

That's not cheap.

"What do you want?" Ann quizzed her. "What has my sister told you?"

Lainey sat down and began her rehearsed story.

"I'm an insurance investigator and Mary found me through a mutual friend. She asked me to research a theory she had about your brother Doug and the Sullivan family." She watched carefully for any reaction from Ann. There was none.

"We aren't close."

"Do you mean you and Mary aren't close?"

"Oh, I see," Ann said sarcastically. "Mary told you I take advantage of Doug, didn't she?"

Lainey didn't want to give away too much information.

"Mary told me about the DNA results showing Doug was a half-brother to you and the Sullivans. She does believe that the deaths of Eugene and Harold may not have been accidents and she is worried for your brother's safety."

Ann sat there with no response. Lainey continued. "Whether you and Mary get along is not my concern, I assure you, and not why I am here."

Again, there was no response from Ann. Lainey thought it was time to bring out a bigger gun.

"I understand that your boyfriend is a part-time body driver with Doug."

Ann's demeanor changed instantly, and Lainey couldn't tell if her look was one of worry or surprise.

"Chuck does drive part-time when the repair business is slow," she said deliberately. "I guess Doug needs extra income, too."

Lainey knew that Ann was either flat out lying or very intelligent…or both.

"Are you close to Doug?" She asked as she took out her iPad to pretend to take notes.

"Since you talked to Mary, you know I am," Ann quipped. "Do you think he works a second job because I ask him for money?"

Now, Lainey knew Ann was smart and sly. She decided not to answer that question and instead pursued a different line. "I know you met with Raymond Sullivan and asked him to give Doug a job as a driver for one of his facilities." She was eager to see how Ann responded to that information.

Without hesitation, Ann answered.

"I did. I knew Doug would never ask. Since Raymond was a blood relative, I asked for him."

The back door opened, and a man walked into the front room. Before Lainey could stand up to introduce herself, Ann blurted out, "Chuck, this lady was sent by Mary."

Lainey knew that was some sort of warning sign to Chuck and he instantly put his guard up.

Chuck stopped in his tracks and said to Ann, "Is she bothering you?"

Ann, looking at Lainey, didn't answer for a second. "It's okay. She's leaving anyway."

Lainey stood up, smiled, put her hand out and said, "Hello. I'm Lainey Maynard. You must be Chuck Austin, the car repair guy." She hoped her friendly tone would ease the tension in the room. But it didn't.

Chuck didn't shake her hand and instead made clear his views. "Unless you have a car problem, you need to leave."

Lainey drew back her hand and picked up her iPad. "Thank you, Ann, for visiting with me," she said as she turned to leave. "And it was nice to meet you, Chuck."

She opened the door and looked back. Ann was still sitting on the couch and Chuck was standing beside her, his hand on her shoulder. "You have a great day," she said and walked out the door.

As Lainey walked to her car, the hair on the back of her neck began to tingle, and she had the distinct feeling she was being watched. She got into the car and tried to look around without raising suspicion. The lights were on in the auto shop and she caught a brief glimpse of a shadow looking through the window of the shop entrance door.

She was almost home when her car Bluetooth rang.

It was Doug Reynolds. "Ann said you went to see her. I don't want her upset by Mary, her ridiculous ideas, or you," Doug began before Lainey could get a word out. "If you need information about Ann, please talk with me. I don't want you going to her house again." There was a commanding note in his voice.

"I'm sorry if I upset you or Ann. I was only with her for a few minutes and only wanted to ask…" Doug interrupted her before she could finish her sentence.

"From now on, if you have any questions, you call me. Ann is to be left alone."

"Yes, I understand. Again, I apologize if I've upset you or Ann."

"I mean it." Doug replied and ended the call.

Well, Ann didn't waste any time calling him now, did she? Wonder what she told him?

Lainey pulled into her garage and was walking in the house when her phone rang again. This time, it was Della.

"Hey." Lainey balanced the phone between her ear and shoulder as she shrugged out of her coat.

"Have you got a minute? Are you home from seeing Ann Reynolds yet?"

Lainey knew Della pretty well and she sensed a hesitation in her voice. "I'm back. What's up?"

"Now, don't be mad, but I told Paul that you needed to talk with him about the Sullivan deaths." Della winced, expecting a loud response from Lainey.

Ugh. Why did she do that?

"I wish you hadn't," Lainey sighed. "What did he say?" She was dreading the answer.

The silence on the phone was deafening. "Paul said to come to his office, and he would try to answer any questions you have."

"Did you explain why I wanted to see his records?"

"I told him about Mary's idea and about what you found out at the police station. He said he would help if he could."

"I'll call him and see if now is a good time."

"I'll go with you if that's okay. If he has reservations about helping, maybe I can influence him. I've made his favorite carrot cake with sour cream frosting. I'll take a piece with us."

Lainey smiled. She agreed, hung up, and called the funeral home.

"Kristiansen Funeral home, may I help you?"

"This is Lainey Maynard. Is Paul available?"

"He left a note that he was expecting a call from you. He said to come by. What time should he expect you?" The polite receptionist inquired.

"Is thirty minutes all right?"

"That should be fine. I'll let him know." The receptionist added, "Have a nice day."

Lainey thanked her. Such a lovely person. She could see why Paul had her answering the phone. She could put anyone at ease. She called Della back to let her know to come as soon as possible.

"I'll meet you there, Lainey. There's no reason for you to drive all the way out here and then back again."

As Lainey drove over to the funeral home, she wondered what information Paul would or could give her.

Would he help if he saw the police report? Had he already seen it?

The two pulled in the parking lot at the same time.

"How fast did you go to get here so quickly?" Lainey asked as they walked in the front door.

Della laughed. "No worries. Paul knows all the law enforcement officers in several counties. And they know I have a lead foot!" She grinned.

Paul was waiting inside the entry hall and greeted them with a hug.

"I see you brought a back-up with you, Lainey…and she brought my favorite dessert to bribe me!" Paul kissed Della on the cheek. "Let's go to my office."

Funeral homes had always made Lainey feel uncomfortable. The elevator-type music that played softly all the time, the strong smell of various types of flowers, the tissue boxes on every end table, the viewing rooms that were so elegantly decorated that they looked as if they came directly from a royal family's bedroom, and the calm, sometimes unnervingly sweet, attitudes of the staff made her skin clammy.

Paul sensed her uneasiness. "Lainey, can I get you something?"

She shuttered slightly, hoping no one noticed. "You wouldn't happen to have any coffee with cream and sugar, would you?"

"Sure," Della said. "I know where the break room is."

"Thanks. I'd appreciate it."

Lainey tried to regroup. She took out the folder she had brought that contained the printed copies of the police reports.

Paul smiled. "This is a place of business like any other office. You can relax." He looked down at the folder she was holding. "Is that the Mary Reynolds information Della told me about?"

Lainey hesitated briefly. "No. It's the police reports for Eugene and Harold Sullivan." She laid the folder on Paul's desk.

"The police reports?" He looked surprised as he opened the file. "How did Mary Reynolds get copies of these?"

She fidgeted in her chair and finally admitted, "Actually, I didn't get those from Mary."

Paul looked directly at her and said, "Who gave you these?"

There was no response.

Paul asked again, "Who gave you these?"

Lainey was still silent.

Paul sighed and said, "Okay. Have you at least spoken with anyone from the police department about this?"

She gave a sigh of relief. "Yes! I spoke with Sarge. I mean Ben Sargent."

"I know Sarge. He's a good man."

She nodded in agreement. Paul took a few minutes to look through both files before he spoke.

"How can I help you?" He asked.

Della had returned with the coffee and was once again sitting next to Lainey.

"Paul, the reports say Doug Reynolds and Chuck Austin were the body drivers for both accidents. And that they brought the bodies here." Lainey moved to the edge of her chair.

"That's right. Doug and Chuck do a lot of driving for me and a couple of the other funeral homes in the area."

"Autopsies weren't ordered for either death. Is that right?"

"Yes, it is. The police report stated that," he answered.

"You have been in this business for many, many years and I'm sure have seen a lot of accidents. After you saw the bodies, did you question why no autopsies were ordered?" She asked, realizing that sounded a bit confusing.

Paul sat back in his high-backed chair. "We get calls to receive deceased persons at all hours of the day and night. Sometimes it can be very hectic with several arriving within a few hours. There are highly regulated policies and procedures concerning the handling, transporting, and receiving of bodies, as well as the procedures to prepare bodies in order to protect the spread of possible viruses, diseases, and such."

"I understand that. You've seen tons of suspicious deaths, with or without injuries, where an autopsy was required. Did you think the injuries to Eugene or Harold should have warranted that an autopsy be requested?"

Paul thought for a moment. "When a body arrives, I have the police report. It includes the findings of the coroner's investigation. If it says that no autopsy is necessary, I don't normally second guess them. I know Nathan Austin. He has been with the coroner's office for years and started out there as a summer intern. "If he found no evidence that would suggest foul play, I believe him."

"Would Nathan Austin be related to Chuck Austin?" Lainey asked.

"He is Chuck's brother."

Lainey grinned and looked at Della.

"I thought they were related!" Della said excitedly.

"Wait! Am I missing something?" Paul asked looking from Della to Lainey and back to Della,

"I think there are a few coincidences that may turn out to NOT be coincidences at all!" Lainey smiled. "Tell me what you think of these facts." She put her elbows on Paul's desk. "Doug Reynolds and his sisters find out he is a half-brother to a family who just happens to own the Sullivan's Best Poultry empire that is worth a fortune. Three living Sullivan brothers are told and acknowledge that Doug is indeed a half-brother and therefore could be an heir to the family fortune. They meet several times and agree to be friends." She stopped to see if he was following.

"Okay," Paul nodded. "Go on."

"Unknown to Doug, his younger sister, Ann, visits Raymond Sullivan and asks for a job for him. Raymond agrees to do so, but Doug refuses and is upset with Ann for asking."

Shaking his head slightly, Paul asked, "What are you getting at?"

"Within a few weeks of these new family reunion meetings, two of the Sullivan brothers die in seemingly unrelated and unfortunate accidents. No autopsy was ordered on either one." Lainey paused for a second. "Did you know that Ann Reynolds lives with Chuck Austin?"

Paul shook his head, "No."

"Did you know that Doug and Chuck were the body drivers for both accidents?" She probed further.

"Yes. I am aware of that."

"Don't you think it odd that Nathan Austin was the investigator from the coroner's office for both?" She asked as if she was giving Paul the third degree.

He picked up the file again, took out two pages, set the folder back down and reread the pages he took out.

"I agree there are some timing coincidences between when the Reynolds's found out about the Sullivans and the two Sullivan brothers' deaths. But that's not evidence that would stand up in court."

Lainey nodded. "Did you happen to keep pictures of Eugene and Harold's injuries or trauma that might have been recorded?"

Paul put down the two pages and looked at her. "Everything is documented, but I don't keep pictures of the bodies on file. The police may have some from the accident scenes. And besides, these two bodies were cremated, so the preparation procedure is completely different."

Lainey slapped her forehead. "So there is no way to go back and reexamine a body if there was a question of murder!"

"That's right," Paul replied.

"I read somewhere that cremation doesn't burn up the entire body or that pieces are left or something like that," Lainey said.

It was Della that shuddered this time. "Yuck. If you don't mind, I think I'll wait in the break room while you talk about this."

"Let me try to explain the process. Can you stomach going back to the retort area?" Paul asked.

Lainey remembered from her research that retort was the official word for the ovens used in cremation. She really didn't want to see one but felt she had to.

"Is someone back there now?" She asked with a slightly weaker voice.

"Only the crematory operator if he is still here."

They walked out a side door in Paul's office. The stark difference in decor surprised Lainey. The bright florescent light of the hallway hurt her eyes. The plain, grey walls and white Styrofoam paneled ceiling tiles were dull and dingy from age. There was no music, no pictures hanging on the walls, no elegant furniture, and no tissue boxes. It was completely empty. A single, solid metal door waited for them at the other end.

Their footsteps echoed loudly. Paul walked up to the door, inserted a code into the key pad lock, and opened the door for Lainey.

Chapter Seven

❧

As Lainey walked into the room, she noticed that the walls were concrete blocks and the ceiling was unfinished. The rust-colored metal support beams showed the metal sheeting roof between them.

She found herself saying to Paul, "This is a commercial warehouse."

He smiled. "Yes, it basically is."

As she looked around the room, she noticed that metal shelving racks framed one side of the area. Each rack had four large shelves. Some shelves had grey or black body bags on them.

Paul must have seen the confusion on Lainey's face. He touched her arm. "If this bothers you, we can talk in my office."

Lainey shook her head no. Her mouth was suddenly

very dry. He motioned for her to walk over to the middle section of the room.

"The racks are where bodies are put when they arrive. Each bag is clearly marked with several identification tags and authorization forms are checked. There are many forms to sign and procedures with which the state requires our compliance. We treat each body with respect. Either another funeral director or I read the reports and then prepare the body as requested."

"What do you mean by prepare the body?"

"We must remove any objects such as pacemakers, metal objects, or IV lines that might explode inside the retort when heated. There have been accidents where explosions inside retorts or during the process of removing the remains that have killed workers."

Lainey nodded, but her gaze was fixed on a wall directly in front of her. The wall had two large steel door openings that were each six feet wide and at least five feet tall. The doors were centered between the floor and the top of the wall. Bricks surrounded each door. It reminded Lainey of outdoor ovens she had seen people install on their patios.

Paul continued. "You are looking at the retorts. These are where the cremation process takes place. We are not standing close to either retort, but can you feel heat coming from them?"

"Yes, from the one on the right," she answered.

"These heat to 2,000 degrees as required by state law. The one on the right is in the cooling down period," Paul explained. "When the retort is being used, the heat radiating from inside makes it impossible to get too close."

Lainey walked toward her left. "And what is that area?"

"Once the required cool down time has passed, the door is opened carefully, and the container holding the remains slides out. There is a door, if you will, under each container. That is opened and the remains are sifted through the screen into the sterile bag."

"You mean the ashes of the person?"

"Well, yes, most of them. There are larger things, pieces of bone, fillings and such that are not completely cremated during the process. These are removed through a second, larger door at the end of the body container. There are strict rules in disposing of these remains as well. They are put in a pulverizer-type machine then discarded."

"Discarded?" She looked at Paul. "How?"

"It sounds a bit harsh, but the remaining residue from the pulverizer is vacuumed out with a shop vac and thrown away." He watched for the appearance of shock on Lainey's face. Everyone that heard that for the first time was shocked. He didn't have to wait long.

"Oh dear!" Lainey gasped. "Thrown away?"

"Yes, we have to dispose of them and clean all the equipment as much as we can."

Lainey thought for a minute and suddenly her thoughts were crystal clear. "That makes it virtually impossible to trace objects or do bone DNA testing, doesn't it?"

Paul nodded. "Yes, it does." They left the retort area and walked down the hallway to his office.

"Were you the one who prepared both of the Sullivans for cremation?" Lainey asked as soon as he sat down.

He looked a bit surprised. "Actually, according to the medical and coroner's reports, there were no objects to consider removing. Lainey, I want to tell you again that nothing looked out of the ordinary. I did prepare both of those bodies."

"I see."

She sat with her back against the chair as Della came back into the office.

"Did you give her the creamery tour?" Della asked as she kissed the top of Paul's head. Lainey laughed out loud.

"It's not a creamery Della....It's a crematory." He chuckled a bit.

"Oh, well, you know what I meant."

"Your hubby was great and I learned a lot. Thank you, Paul," Lainey acknowledged with a half-smile and nod.

"Ladies, I do have another appointment. If I can help you, Lainey, please call me. Della, my love, I'll see you at home around seven."

The two friends left the funeral home and stopped to talk at Lainey's car.

"Well?" Della asked. "You still think murder?"

"Yes, ma'am, I certainly do!" Lainey said confidently. "I plan on telling Sarge this evening about my findings and see what he has to say."

"Call me. I'm eager to hear!"

Lainey drove home and had a couple of hours before she was to meet Sarge. Something Paul said was nagging at her.

"...IV lines if a person had been ill," she said aloud.

She started her computer and when the Google search page loaded, she clicked on the microphone icon and said, "Medical devices that must be removed before cremation."

Thousands of links appeared, and Lainey spent the next hour reading through them. She found an education link that dealt with funeral director training for cremation procedures. The link included a list of commonly used chemical materials that needed to be removed when preparing a body. Searching through the alphabetic listing of the materials and other treatments given to terminally ill patients, her eyes and her mind focused on one entry.

"Fentanyl Patches," she said to herself. Looking at

her watch and realizing she had to leave for her meeting with Sarge, she quickly printed out the pages relating to the patches.

"Let's see what he says about this!" She said as she put the printed pages into her already bulging folder.

Lainey walked into the police station on the dot at 8 p.m. The receptionist buzzed Sarge who came to the front to meet her.

"Look familiar?" He asked as the two walked down the hallway toward his office.

That startled her. *Had he seen her last evening? Why would he ask that?*

"I'm not sure I have been in the back of the station before," she hoped to not sound like she was lying.

They walked into his office and he pointed at a chair directly in front of his desk. "Have a seat."

Suddenly, she felt like she was being interrogated and her senses went on high alert.

Think before you speak.

She smiled and waited for Sarge to say something. It seemed like hours before he said, "Francy mentioned this was about the Sullivan cases."

Taking a breath, Lainey began. "I know you told me that nothing looked suspicious, but I think I have evidence that might change your mind."

She waited for his reaction. His swivel chair squeaked as he leaned back and looked at her. "I assume this evidence is in the folder you are holding?" he asked.

She nodded and opened the folder to find the fentanyl patch papers. When she handed them to him, Sarge said, "No, I want to see the entire folder."

Lainey felt trapped. She knew the police report copies were still in the folder and once he saw them, she was caught.

She hesitated, put the printed pages back and hoping that honesty would somehow lessen the trouble she might be in, handed Sarge the folder.

"I came here last evening with Francy's Mom and got copies of the police reports for the Sullivan cases." Her chest felt heavy and she tried to breath slowly to calm down.

Sarge didn't respond and took what seemed like hours to look through the folder.

"I met with Paul Kristiansen today and he explained to me the cremation process. Since both bodies were cremated, there is no way to do any further testing."

Sarge looked at her, nodded, and looked back down at the papers without saying a word. She knew that Law Enforcement officials used the quiet treatment many times to make suspects nervous enough to start talking and incriminate themselves. In fact, she had done that at times while investigating a case.

She leaned back in her chair and crossed her arms in front of her, deciding to wait him out. *I'm not saying anything until he speaks first.* Minutes passed and Lainey tried not to fidget or move at all. Finally, Sarge leaned forward in his chair and put the folder on his desk. He was holding a few papers in his hand.

"I saw your car when I came to let you in and knew it was the same car Vera supposedly borrowed last evening." He looked directly at her. "I don't know you very well, but I do know and respect Francy. She wouldn't put herself in danger by helping you if she didn't feel there was some merit in your concerns. And everyone loves Vera, but normally when she brought treats to the office, she and Francy were planning a vacation and needed approval for the days off," he continued, and a small smile appeared on his face.

"I am not pleased that you found the reports and took copies from this office. You do know I could arrest you and put you in jail, right? But since technically you did not break in, and I trust Francy, I'm going to overlook it this time," he scolded.

Lainey felt her shoulders relax a bit. Whether it was nerves or a bad sense of comedic timing, she instantly replied, "But didn't Vera's goodies taste great?"

Sarge put down the papers he was holding and after a second, smiled. "Yes, they always are. Help me tie your notes, the reports, and your cremation details together with Fentanyl patches," he stated.

She let out a big breath. "On the police reports, do

you see that Doug Reynolds and Chuck Austin were body drivers on both cases?"

He nodded.

"Do you know that Nathan Austin, the investigator from the coroner's office on both cases, is the brother of Chuck Austin?"

He didn't respond.

Lainey continued. "Chuck Austin is the boyfriend of Ann Reynolds, Doug's youngest sister."

With that bit of news, Sarge spoke up. "I see. No, I was not aware of that relationship." He again sat back in his chair in deep thought."If there is something suspicious in these cases, the information you shared seems to implicate Doug Reynolds as well."

Lainey tried to put all her findings in a brief summary for Sarge. She began telling him about Ann's disabilities, Doug's guilt about the accident that killed their father, and how dependent Ann seems to be on Doug's financial support.

She also pointed to the family notes stating that Doug and the Sullivan brothers had met, became somewhat friends, and that Ann had asked for a job for Doug. She ended by saying that Doug was very upset with Ann and refused to take any money from the Sullivan family.

"I spoke with Ann today and not only was she unfriendly, but she was also arrogant and abrupt.

When Chuck Austin came into the room and ordered me to leave, Ann immediately called Doug."

Sarge had been listening intently. "If, and I'm not saying there is, but if one or more of these people are involved in the deaths of Eugene and Harold, how do you tie in the patches?"

"When I talked with Paul, he mentioned that bodies have to be prepared for cremation and all metal objects like pacemakers and metal plates have to be removed by the mortician in order to prevent explosions during the heating period." She hoped that he might be impressed with her knowledge.

"I know that," Sarge replied. "But that doesn't tie in to the patches."

"Paul said that medical IV's and other devices on a body would also be removed. The pages I printed out from a reputable source said that Fentanyl patches are highly toxic even after being used or stuck to the skin."

He nodded. "We have dealt with deaths reported of children, pets, and drug addicts being exposed to the powder or gel on these type of patches. Some terminal cancer patients will put too many patches on in order to end their suffering. Death occurs within a short time even with very minimal exposure to this substance."

Lainey sighed. "With all this, would you say there is enough evidence to perhaps open the case for further investigation?"

Sarge shook his head. "I'm afraid not. We would

need more concrete proof that a person or persons had access to these patches and used them to somehow poison both Sullivan brothers. As it stands right now, none of your evidence would fly in court. A defense attorney would have this all thrown out as hearsay and theory."

Lainey frowned. "I need more proof," she muttered softly.

"I will say that there are many coincidences in these cases. But where or what is the hard evidence?"

"I'll find it."

"I have to caution you, Lainey, that you are not protected under the law as there is no legal investigation going on. And if these two deaths were murder and not accidental, the guilty parties are not going to be pleased with you snooping around."

She had already thought of that. "Can you help me?"

Sarge paused a long while. "I'll do a little investigating off the record for you and that's it. Francy said you were a good investigator and I can see that you are determined. I remind you not to break the law and want your promise that you will call me BEFORE you get yourself involved in a possibly dangerous situation. I'm not joking. Call me first."

"I promise to keep you updated on anything I find."

Sarge nodded in agreement. Lainey thanked him and stood to leave. As she reached the door, he added another stern warning that chilled her to the bone.

"Call me FIRST," He emphasized the last word so hard, a few spit dots spewed out of his mouth and floated down to the floor.

"I will, I will," she assured him.

For another night, Lainey could not sleep. Was she jumping to ludicrous conclusions that somehow Ann and the Austins' had committed the murders? Or was it simply a coincidence of the brothers' deaths and the contemptuous attitude of Ann and her boyfriend? Was Doug involved, too?

It was 6:30 a.m. and she decided to drive to the coffee house, get a large coffee before starting to work. As she sat in front of her computer, coffee in hand, she thought aloud. "Think, Lainey! How could Chuck get his hands on Fentanyl patches? And how could the Sullivan brothers be exposed to them?"

Hours passed as she searched online, made notes, and drank her coffee. Sarge had said she needed hard evidence and she knew she would need help to get that type of evidence. Her thoughts turned to Mary. If anyone was likely to help her, it might just be Mary.

She picked up the phone and called Mary's cell.

"Hello," Mary answered. "Is this Lainey?"

"Why, yes it is, Mary. Did my name appear on your phone?"

"I added you to my phone contacts," Mary said. "I only answer calls if I know the person's name. Have you found something to help Doug?"

"I have a theory, and have spoken with the police department, but I need to find hard evidence before they can do anything more." She paused. "And I think I can do that with your help."

"What do you need me to do?" Mary asked eagerly.

"I have to warn you that it could be dangerous if we are caught and I'm not sure we would have police support if they knew what we were doing. Do you still want to help me?"

"If it will help Doug, yes."

"Good. I do think that Ann, Chuck, and perhaps his brother, Nathan, are involved in the Sullivan brothers' deaths. What I want to do is get into Chuck's garage and see if I can find the evidence I need."

"You mean schedule an appointment with him to fix your car or something?"

"Not exactly. When I talked with Ann, Chuck came into the house while I was there. He knows my face and who I am. He would find it suspicious if I call to have my car repaired. I've got to get in after dark or when the shop is empty."

"I see," Mary said. "And how do you want me to help you?"

"How often does Ann leave the house? I mean does she go shopping or out to eat?"

"You know that I am not close to Ann."

"Do you know anything about Chuck's activities?

When he has errands or might be out of the shop?" Lainey continued, writing down notes.

"My friend is a waitress at the VFW in town and says Chuck comes there about 6 p.m. every night when he is not on a call from the coroner's office. He's a regular."

"Do you think you could get Ann away from the house tonight at the same time Chuck is at the VFW?"

Mary was silent.

"I know you don't get along, but is there anything you can do to get her away from the house while I get into the garage and look around?"

Lainey could hear Mary sigh. "I can't promise to get her out of the house, but I can try to get her distracted enough not to notice anything in the shop."

"May I ask how?" Lainey probed.

"I'll go to her house unexpectedly a little after 6 to talk with her about Doug's life insurance policy. She will let me in to talk about that."

Lainey's ears perked up. "Doug's life insurance policy?"

"Yes. Ann and I are his beneficiaries. Ann has been after me to sign over my half to her. I'll tell her I'm ready to talk about that." Mary's voice sounded angry as she mentioned her sister's name.

Lainey's thoughts went to how much inheritance Doug would receive now that he was a Sullivan relative and her goose bumps returned. She suddenly realized that she needed to be cautious around Mary, too. Even half of the Sullivan estate would be a huge fortune.

"I know it will be difficult, but this could provide us with the evidence we need."

"I'm doing this for Doug and no one else," Mary said determinedly.

Lainey thought for a moment. "We will go to Ann's house. When you go inside to talk with her, I'll slip over to the shop and look around."

"Want me to pick up you around 5:30?" Mary asked.

Lainey had been trained to always leave herself another way out of any situation and riding in Mary's car would make her completely dependent on her. "I'll drive over to your house and follow you to Ann's. I can park down the road and never be seen."

"Sounds good. I'll see you here by 5:30."

Lainey clicked off her phone. Her instinct was to call Sarge and let him know of her plan, but she decided not to. "It's better to ask for forgiveness after the fact than try to get permission beforehand," she chuckled to herself.

Chapter Eight

Lainey was catching up on emails and completing paperwork for a couple of cases she had been assigned when her cell phone rang. The caller ID showed it to be a private caller. She had been getting so many robocalls that she usually didn't answer and blocked the number from calling again. But something told her to pick it up this time.

"Hello?"

"Is this Lainey Maynard?" The somewhat familiar voice answered.

"Yes, it is. May I help you?"

"This is Raymond Sullivan," he began. "I think my life has been threatened and I want you to investigate."

She swallowed hard. "Threatened? How?"

"I'd rather not discuss this over the phone. I am

heading to our plant in Cokato and will be there in about 30 minutes. How long will it take you to get there?"

"I'll be there in under an hour."

She quickly got her things together and headed to the plant. She was thankful that no police were monitoring the 60 mph speed limit on Hwy 12 this morning as she pushed her cruise up to 80.

She arrived at the plant main entrance, pushed the intercom to give her name, and the door was instantly unlocked.

As she walked into the reception area, a security guard stopped her to ask for her ID. She handed him her driver's license. He checked the name against a log book and handed back her license.

"Mr. Sullivan is waiting for you. Please, follow me."

She obediently followed through several electronically locked doors and into a large conference room.

Sitting at one end of the long, hardwood table was Raymond Sullivan. He was holding what looked like a medium-sized cup of coffee.

"Please, come in Lainey," Raymond said motioning for the guard to leave. "I thought you might like coffee."

She smiled before she caught herself. *Stick to business, Lainey. Don't get distracted.*

"That was very kind, Raymond, and certainly not

necessary. I do appreciate it," she said as she sat down in the chair next to him.

He nodded and smiled. "I believe it is a sugar-free mocha Frappuccino."

She smiled again. "What happened to make you think your life has been threatened?"

"In many of our poultry stores or at the plant sites, we have a small museum detailing a brief history of Sullivan's Best Poultry and how the products have evolved over the years. We have a few T-shirts and novelty items visitors can purchase, but they are there to promote goodwill and to thank people in our communities."

"I see," she said as she took notes on her iPad.

"In the flagship museum is my Dad's first poultry delivery truck. We like to drive it in local parades from time to time and therefore keep it in good running condition..." he paused.

Lainey looked up. "I'm sorry, Raymond. I *am* listening, but I like to keep good notes," she said apologetically.

He nodded and continued. "A plant manager took it in for repairs a few days ago and I was driving it back to the museum yesterday afternoon."

Lainey purposely stopped writing to look into Raymond's eyes. She saw worry, maybe fear.

"I noticed the truck was not handling like it always did. Something was different about the acceleration of the engine when I would come to a stop. I was close to my home and took the truck into my personal auto mechanic. They put the truck on their diagnostic machine and found that the brakes and accelerator had been modified and were malfunctioning." He sat forward and waited for Lainey to respond.

"Did the mechanic think it was an error or fault of the repairman? What machine shop did the work?"

Raymond hesitated before stating, "My mechanic says it was intentional. And the shop that did the work was Austin's Bang or Bump."

Lainey's jaw dropped open. "As in Chuck Austin's Bang or Bump shop?"

He nodded. "An odd coincidence?"

"I don't know. Is that the shop that always works on the truck?"

"No, it was taken there because it was close to the plant where it had been stored for the holiday parades."

Lainey paused briefly. "I have spoken to Ben Sargent, a respected local law enforcement professional concerning Mary Reynolds Chase's thoughts about your brothers being murdered. I think we need to call him and let him know of this. Will that be all right with you?"

Raymond hesitated. "I still am not totally convinced of the idea of planned murders, but I am also not a person who buries their head in the sand, either. At this point, it is not in my or the company's best interest to become fodder for the tabloids or news stations unnecessarily."

"I understand. I am sure that Sarge would never jeopardize your privacy. May I have your permission to call him? Would you be willing to speak with him?"

"All right." He wrote down his personal cell phone number and handed it to her. "Please have him call this number only. Not my office."

"Of course." Then she added, "Please, do not drive or touch the car until you have spoken with Sarge. I think he may want to look at it as well."

He nodded. "Thank you for coming on short notice."

"Not a problem. Please, call me anytime." Lainey stood, extending her hand to shake Raymond's, making sure not to tip over the coffee cup still sitting the table.

He shook her hand. "I will look for your friend's call." He opened the door and she walked out with her iPad and coffee.

Feeling more confident that she was getting solid evidence for Sarge, she hurried down the hallway. As she was walking past the security guard's desk, she turned slightly, intending to thank him. Instead, as she turned, her elbow bumped the edge of the desk and her coffee cup once again was emptied onto the floor.

"Oh, I am terribly sorry!" she muttered to the guard. The guard shook his head. "It's quite all right. Mr.

Sullivan said to have a janitor handy while you were in the building."

Lainey felt her face flush. She embarrassingly hurried out the front door, leaving the cup and coffee on the floor behind her. She started her car and immediately called Sarge. He was silent for a moment after she had told him the details Raymond shared with her. She did not mention the possible life insurance beneficiary connection with the case nor her plan to sneak into Chuck's repair shop and look around.

"I want to speak with Raymond as soon as possible," Sarge said and added, "This information could provide evidence to reopen the Sullivan deaths. But I caution you that I said *could* provide. Let's not count our chickens before they hatch."

She tried to quell the excitement in her voice. "I understand."

"And Lainey," Sarge said with that deep, scolding tone in his voice, "Don't do any more investigating until I contact you. Is that clear? It could be dangerous."

"Of course." Lainey lied. Searching Austin's shop was more important than ever and nothing, not even a stern warning from Sarge, would stop her from going this evening.

She drove up to Mary's house a few minutes early and Mary was waiting for her.

"Are you sure you want to do this?" She asked.

The scowl on Mary's face said it was not going to be

a pleasant experience. "Let's get this over with," she sighed as she walked to her car. "I'm doing this for Doug."

"I will park away from the sight line of Ann's front door and wait behind the trees until I see you go inside."

Mary nodded. "How will you know when I am leaving?"

That is something Lainey had been thinking about all day. What kind of signal could Mary give that she could hear if she was still inside the shop?

"Are you taking your cell phone?" Lainey asked.

"Yes," Mary replied.

"Type my cell phone number in as if you were going to call. Then when you leave, hit the call button as soon as possible. If I'm not in my car as you drive past, wait fifteen minutes to hear from me."

"What if I don't hear from you in fifteen minutes?"

"Call Sarge at the police station. Tell him where I am and that I may need help."

Mary had a worried look on her face. "What happens if you get caught in the shop? Or if I can't reach Sarge?"

Lainey swallowed hard. "If Sarge doesn't answer, call 911."

The thick woods on either side of the road to Ann's cabin allowed no light to shine through and the blackness made the early evening hour seem like midnight.

Lainey parked her car on the main road a block away from the house. As she walked down the dark, snowy driveway, she could see Mary getting out of her car. She stood behind a clump of trees where she could see the front door and the shop.

Mary knocked on the door and even from a distance, Lainey could hear the conversation.

"What are you doing here?" Ann asked as she opened the door.

Mary, standing very upright replied, "I want to talk about Doug's will." For a moment, both women stood glaring at each other and Lainey thought Ann might slam the door in her face.

Finally, Mary walked into the house. Lainey wasted no time and ran over to the shop.

Now to find a way in!

She tried the front door. It was locked as were the front two windows. Lainey crept along the side of the shop and found a back entrance. Sure enough, it was open. She turned on her cell phone flashlight, pointed it toward the ground and walked in.

The smell of gasoline, motor oil, and grease stung her nose. Inside the large room were a couple of cars on lifts surrounded by various machines, tools, and electric cords. Metal storage cabinets lined one outside wall and she noticed a small paint booth area in the opposite corner.

Toward the front of the building was a large walled-off section that she thought was the office. As she walked toward the room, she tripped over a large trash can and the loud clanging noise it made as it hit the cement floor made her heart skip a beat.

"I hope no one heard that!" She bent down to pick up the can and the trash that had spilled out.

"Old Chuck must like Burger King a lot," she said to herself as she picked up a dozen or so empty burger boxes. She looked around once more before going inside the office just to make sure no one had entered. Once inside, since the room had no windows, she shut the door and turned on the light switch.

The room had been sectioned off with the first area as the check-in space. She walked behind the counter and saw it was covered with dirt, grease, clipboards, pens, and newspapers. There were no filing cabinets or anything Lainey could use.

She opened the door behind the counter into what looked like Chuck's office. She sat in his desk chair and hurriedly looked through the desk drawers. Besides being full of tire pressure gages, pens, keychains, and scraps of paper, Lainey found nothing that would be evidence of any kind.

She thought for a moment. "Where would I hide evidence if I was going to murder someone?" she said aloud, looking around again to see if she had missed something.

The walls were covered with pictures of all sizes of racing cars and drivers. Lainey walked over to look at them and saw that Chuck was standing with the drivers in several of them. It was then that she noticed one of the pictures was not of a race car and was hanging a bit crooked.

"Now why would Chuck put a picture of a fishing boat in the middle of a bunch of race cars?" she thought. When she tried to take the picture off the wall for a closer look, it wouldn't budge. She pulled harder and turned it to the right to help loosen it.

She heard a loud 'click' behind her as she turned the picture. Turning around quickly, she saw a small door opening behind the desk that she had not noticed before. This door only had handles on the inside. She pulled the door open and what she saw made her skin crawl.

"Holy smokes," Lainey exclaimed as she stood facing a tilted gurney with large examination lights hanging above it. She saw a metal operating room tray with instruments on it, boxes of disposable gloves and boxes of plastic sandwich bags. The horrific realization hit her. "It's a small autopsy room!" She gasped.

Her heart was racing. She started taking pictures with her phone camera and noticed a couple of hazardous waste containers. She grabbed a paper towel and opened the first one. She snapped a couple of pictures of the contents and then she stopped dead in her tracks.

The light she had turned on when she entered the front part of the office suddenly shut off and the only light visible was her cell phone. She quickly turned off her flashlight and ducked under the exam table to hide. She hardly breathed and her heart pounded wildly inside her chest.

Lainey was afraid the light from her phone would bring the person directly to her if she tried to call or text for help. So she waited. She heard no footsteps or voices. Tiny beads of sweat trickled down her forehead into her eyes. She didn't dare look at her phone to see how much time had passed since the light was turned off, although it felt like hours. Was Mary still inside the house? Or did she see that Lainey was not in her car if she had left? Would she call Sarge if she hadn't heard from her fifteen minutes after that?

Lainey's mind was racing as she fought herself to stay calm and still. More time passed and she knew she had to do something. She turned on her cell phone and sent a text to Mary. "Are you still in the house? I'm still in the shop!"

Mary did not respond. After a few minutes more, Lainey knew she had to get out of the shop. She slowly got out from under the table, grabbed one of the small waste containers and made her way back through the hidden door, the office and the shop area to the back door she had entered. She saw no one.

Once she was outside, she looked at the cabin and saw that Mary was walking to her car. Lainey waited for her to back out and once her car lights were gone, she ran back to where her car was parked. Safely inside her car, her cell phone rang, and it was Mary.

"You need to get out of the shop! I'm on my way home!" Mary was shouting into the phone.

"Mary, it's okay. I'm in my car and heading back to my house," she said as calmly as she could, but she knew her voice was shaking.

"What did you find? You sound scared. What happened?" She probed Lainey for answers.

"I'm fine. I don't know for sure what I found and need to regroup. How did it go with Ann?"

"She is deviously cunning, and it was obvious she told nothing but lies to me. I told her I had to think before signing over my share of Doug's life insurance to her." Mary said angrily. "It'll be a cold day in hades before I speak to her again."

"I understand and appreciate your help. Once I find out anything, I will let you know."

When Lainey got inside her own home, she didn't reach for coffee this time. She sat down with Powie on her lap, took in a deep breath, and tried to relax. Suddenly the fear, anxiety, and sheer terror she had been hiding inside overwhelmed her and her eyes burned as tears rolled down her cheeks.

"Pull it together, Lainey!" She scolded herself. "You're okay." She kept wondering who could have turned the light off in Chuck's office. Suddenly it dawned on her that the light must have been on a timer!

"Of course!" she exclaimed aloud. "It's like my utility room light. Once turned on, it turns off automatically after a certain length of time!" The ring of her cell phone startled her. She looked at the caller ID. It was Sarge.

"Hello, Sarge," she said. "Did you speak to Raymond?"

"This is not a social call." Sarge blasted his voice into the phone. "Did I not tell you to stop snooping around on this case?"

Lainey was not expecting that and did not answer him right away.

"Ann Reynolds has just called in a complaint of someone very similar to your description breaking into their auto shop this evening." He said angrily.

Lainey's mind was racing. She knew Sarge would not settle for any excuses trying to hide things. She took a deep breath in and said, "Did she see anyone?"

He didn't answer.

"Do you have evidence of someone breaking

inside?" she asked Sarge again, not wanting to admit to anything just yet.

"She doesn't have hard evidence, but thought she saw a woman running down her driveway toward the street carrying something." He stated flatly. "Does that happen to ring a bell with you?"

Lainey was silent.

Sarge responded by saying, "Be at my office in fifteen minutes." And then he added, "Bring whatever it was you took from there." And he hung up.

Chapter Nine

Sarge was waiting in the police station reception area when Lainey entered.

"Hello, Sarge," Lainey greeted. He simply nodded, knocked on the window for the dispatcher to open the door, and motioned for her to go inside.

She followed him in silence down the now familiar hallway to his office. Once inside, he closed the door and sat down behind his desk. As a kind of peace offering, Lainey put the waste container she took from Chuck Austin's shop on his desk and sat down. The stony expression on Sarge's face did not change and for several moments the two people stared at each other.

"You blinked first!" she smiled, pointing her finger at him and said teasingly, trying to lighten the mood.

"This is not a game, Lainey!" Sarge barked as he stood with his hands on his hips. "What in Heaven's name do you think you were doing? Do you realize the danger you were in or the position you put me in?" He paced back and forth.

She dared not move or speak. She was trying to find the right words to answer his questions.

"Are Francy and Vera involved again?" He continued to grill her. "What about Della or Paul? Have you dragged them into this, too?" Sarge stopped pacing and was again standing behind his desk facing her.

Lainey realized she had been wiggling in her chair, crossing one leg over the other and back the entire time he was speaking.

"Sarge, I know you are upset, and I apologize if I have put you in an unpleasant situation," she said in the most apologetic voice she could muster.

He didn't move or respond.

She continued, "I did go out to Ann's cabin and I did go into the auto shop to look around. But I did not break in! The back door was unlocked."

Sarge sat down in his chair and stared intently at Lainey.

She pulled out her telephone. "Chuck has an autopsy room hidden in that shop. I have pictures to prove it." She blurted out excitedly.

His expression changed to one of disbelief. "What? That's impossible," he said as he took her phone to examine the pictures.

Lainey, feeling less like a convicted criminal than a

few minutes ago, continued. "I also took pictures of the material in the waste container I left behind."

While he flipped through her cell phone pictures, she told him how Mary distracted Ann and how she had found the hidden room switch behind a boat picture on the wall in Chuck's shop.

Sarge put down her phone. The stern look on his face had softened. He said, "I need these pictures as evidence. If what I saw in the photos of the waste container contents is the same as what is in this waste container on my desk, we have evidence." He looked at Lainey who was grinning.

"See! I knew it!" She said triumphantly. "Let's see what is in this container." She started to pick it up to open it.

"No! Don't touch that!" He commanded. "It's evidence that I am sending to the lab. If my guess is correct, the contents inside could be extremely toxic. Did you touch any of the contents you saw in either of these containers?"

Lainey shook her head no.

"Good," Sarge said and seemed to relax a bit.

"Wait. What do you think is inside?" She asked hesitantly.

"Used Fentanyl patches, among other things."

Lainey could feel the blood rush from her face to her feet. She knew how deadly any contact with these types of patches could be. "And I've been carrying this container around," she mumbled in shock.

"Exactly. Are you all right? Did anyone else touch or come into contact with this container?"

"No, I left it in my car."

Sarge picked up his phone and called the police lab to come for the container. "Let's go into the clerk's office while we wait for the lab techs to come. I don't want any accidental exposure to this container."

She followed him into the office and sat down, visibly shaken at the thought of how close she came to being exposed to such a deadly substance.

"And before you ask, I did speak with Raymond Sullivan," Sarge sat down. "We want to get a closer look at the truck and talk to Raymond's regular mechanic."

"This means the investigation is open again into the two Sullivan murders?"

Sarge hesitantly said, "We are investigating several events that may be related to the deaths," he paused. "But there could be reasonable doubt that the two deaths were accidental."

"What do we do next?"

"*WE* do nothing," he quickly answered. "This is a police investigation now." He watched the smirk appear on her face.

"I know Chuck somehow murdered the Sullivan brothers and I think Ann planned the whole thing," Lainey grumbled. "I can help you investigate."

He didn't reply, only stared at her.

She continued to plead her case. "What about the autopsy room in Chuck's shop? What about looking at the fish house where Harold died..." suddenly her voice trailed off and it was as if a lightning bolt struck her.

"Holy smokes!" Lainey exclaimed. "That boat in the picture I saw on the wall at Chuck's office was parked next to a fish house!"

His eyes opened wide. "I'm going to get a search warrant for the auto shop. In the meantime, you stay away from both Ann and Chuck. Hear me?"

She went home and for the first time in several nights, she slept soundly. She awoke feeling somewhat proud of herself about the events of last evening and her talk with Sarge. She took a long shower, fixed her hair, and splurged on breakfast by cooking a Mediterranean omelet complete with her favorite olives and feta cheese. Her phone rang as she was cleaning up the dishes.

"Hello, this is Lainey," she answered as she shut the dishwasher door.

She heard a scratchy, muffled voice screaming, "Help me, help me! Ann is trying to kill me!" and the phone went dead.

"Hello? Who is this? Hello?" She looked at the caller ID. Mary Reynolds Chase.

She grabbed her purse and keys and headed to

Mary's house. Thoughts were running wild in her mind. Did Ann know that Lainey was the person at the shop last night? Was it Mary's voice on the phone? Should she call Sarge?

She decided to call Francy first. *If there is trouble, Francy will contact Sarge.*

Francy didn't answer and Lainey left a short, hurried message that Mary Chase was in trouble, that she was on her way to Mary's house, and if she hadn't heard from Lainey in an hour, to call Sarge.

She pulled into Mary's driveway and noticed there were no cars in sight. "What can I use for protection if I need to?" she thought while she looked around the car. She spotted her extra-long ice scraper, grabbed it, and headed to the front door.

Lainey knocked and called out several times, but no answer. There were no lights on that she could see in the front of the house.

Carefully she walked around the house to the back door. As she started to open the screen door, she felt someone's hand cover her mouth and nose. She struggled against the pungent gasoline odor that was burning her nose and throat as she tried to breathe. Then, everything went black.

When she awoke, her head was pounding. She couldn't get her bearings and the bright lights in the room made it difficult for her to open her eyes. Her arms felt so heavy and when she tried to sit up, the room started spinning. She moaned and tried to lay still.

"Well, our nosey problem child is waking up!" Lainey heard a man's voice say.

"Can we finish this now?" Another man's voice said impatiently. "She's a royal pain and the sooner we deal with her the better."

She tried again to open her eyes. Her vision was blurry, but it looked like she was in a very large room. The glaring light came from several round lights fixed above where she was laying. The smell of gasoline still stung her nose and throat when she tried to speak.

"Where am I?" She asked as she tried to sit up again. The throbbing pain from her head forced her to lie down once more.

"Your vision will clear, but your head will most likely hurt for a while longer," the male voice said.

Lainey blinked and tried focusing in the direction of the voice. She saw the outline of a tall man standing close to her. "Who are you?"

"I don't believe we have had the pleasure of meeting. I'm Nathan Austin. And you are Lainey Maynard."

She slowly moved her head back and forth and said, "Nathan Austin? Chuck Austin?"

"My, you are an intelligent one, aren't you?" He said sarcastically. "Yes, I'm Nathan, and this is my brother,

Chuck. I believe you met him at Ann's house." He looked down at Lainey whose eyes had closed again.

"She's coming around. Next time she wakes up, we won't be so cordial," Nathan said to Chuck. "Better tie her hands and feet to the table to be safe."

Chuck nodded. He fastened the straps attached to the table across her wrists and feet. "Let's see her get off here now!"

Thirty minutes had passed before Lainey started to wake up once more. Her head was still hurting and she was very cold. She tried to sit up and realized her hands were tied down.

"What's happening?" She asked as she squirmed, trying to twist out of the straps. "Why am I tied down?"

She moved her head from side to side, looking around the best she could to try and figure out where she was. Then horrific panic hit her. She was in an exam room in the county morgue! That's why she was so cold! Instinctively she yelled for help.

"Help! Is anyone there? I'm alive! Help!" She shouted.

"Stop struggling and screaming. Do you really think anyone is going to hear you?" Chuck Austin sneered. He had walked over to the table and wrapped his fingers around her chin and squeezed.

"I should have snapped your neck when I could have," he said coldly.

"Don't leave bruise marks on her lovely face,

brother," Nathan said. "We don't want any suspicious looking injuries for a coroner to find." He chuckled.

Lainey was regaining her wits and said sharply, "It doesn't take much for a man to hurt a woman when she is strapped down on an exam table!"

Chuck's temper flared and he slapped Lainey so hard her face stung as if she had been burned.

"Keep your smart mouth shut or the next time I'll cut out your tongue!" Chuck yelled.

She glared at him and said nothing. She was praying that Francy had gotten her phone message and called Sarge.

Nathan was standing next to Lainey's right hand where she could clearly see his face.

"I'm sure you have a few questions that you would like to ask me," Nathan snickered. "When you ask, please remember to hold your tongue if you know what I mean." He smiled and looked at Chuck.

Lainey nodded. Her face still stung from his slap.

"Would you please untie me and let me sit up to talk?"

"No," Nathan answered.

"Can I at least get a blanket? I'm freezing."

Nathan looked at Chuck and nodded in the direction of a cabinet. Chuck got a blanket and threw it on her legs.

"Thank you."

"So much for the polite banter. We don't...or I

should say, you don't, have much time," Nathan said as he rolled a shiny metal instrument table toward him.

"How did you murder Eugene and Harold Sullivan?" Lainey asked bluntly.

"My, we are direct, aren't we?" Nathan responded seemingly amused by her bluntness.

"The act of murder is easy and frankly somewhat dull. What takes talent and real ingenuity is the planning, preparation, and execution of the plan so as not to get caught." He smiled. "And that is the exciting part of murder!" He looked at Lainey as if waiting for her to praise him for his efforts.

"Ann must have told you about the DNA tests showing Doug was a brother to the Sullivan's. How else would you have known?" She was praying for a miracle that someone would figure out she was here. Keeping Nathan talking would buy her some time.

Chuck, who had been pacing around the room suddenly answered, "Ann's smart. She knew Nathan could help us get the money."

Nathan shot Chuck a glance that even Lainey knew meant to shut up.

"Ann is indeed a bright young girl. Too bad about the accident Doug caused in her early life," Nathan said, mockingly. "It's no wonder he would make her the beneficiary of his life insurance policy."

"So, once the Sullivan fortune came into play, you all saw dollars signs, right?" Lainey stated disgustedly.

Nathan laughed. "That was a perk for sure. You see, we had planned to murder Doug well before any Sullivan DNA tests were done." He picked up on the surprised look on Lainey's face.

"Yes, Doug was going to meet an untimely death, leaving his farm and his large life insurance policy to be split between Ann and us," Nathan said.

"Did you forget that Mary was also an heir to Doug's will?" Lainey asked.

"Did I forget to mention that both Doug and Mary were to be killed in the same unfortunate accident?" Nathan grinned. "You didn't think that I had a plan to get rid of both Doug and Mary? You disappoint me, Lainey."

She was stunned. "You are very intelligent, Nathan."

Chuck was growing more and more impatient. "Can we stop with the questions and just kill her?"

Nathan looked at his watch and then at Lainey. "It is indeed getting late, so if you have no more questions…" he took a pair of gloves off the metal instrument table and began putting them on.

Lainey, trying not to let her fear show in her voice asked, "How did you kill the Sullivan brothers? Did Chuck tamper with Eugene's car? What about Harold?"

Nathan kept putting on his gloves. "It's really very simple. I'm an assistant coroner and therefore am called out to investigate deaths. Chuck has been a body driver for years and when Doug asked to help for extra money, it was perfect."

She watched with wide eyes as Nathan began looking through items on the tray.

"Have you heard of Fentanyl patches?" Nathan asked. "They are quite popular with drug addicts, cancer patients, and the like. And they are quite deadly if used in the wrong way."

Chuck moved closer to the table and was also watching Nathan.

"You see, when I get called to scenes where a death has occurred, I have to examine the body to determine if there might be reasons to suspect foul play or murder, if you will." He grinned. "If the body had Fentanyl patches on it, they stayed on it until it got to the funeral home for processing. I would call Chuck to be the body driver and we would take it to his shop where we removed the Fentanyl patches carefully and then he delivered the body to the funeral home." He stopped and looked at Lainey.

"But you know that since you were in Chuck's shop and saw our little workroom." He stared at her. "That's why you are here in my workroom now."

Lainey couldn't even blink. Her stomach was in knots. "Neither Eugene nor Harold were cancer patients or drug users. How did you..." she was interrupted mid-sentence.

"For someone with a smart mouth, you don't know much, do you?" Chuck sneered.

Lainey thought he was going to hit her again.

"Once Ann found out about the Sullivan connection to Doug, she went to speak with Mr. Raymond Sullivan," Nathan continued. "She not only asked for a job for Doug, but she asked if Chuck could work on their cars. Her pathetic portrayal of the disabled woman worked perfectly! The first time Eugene needed an oil change, he brought it to Chuck."

"Chuck tampered with Eugene's car causing it to crash," Lainey surmised.

"Not at all," Nathan said. "Chuck did the oil change, but he added a few enhancements to the steering wheel, the shifter, and the radio dials."

Chuck smiled at Nathan. "That was too easy."

"Lainey, did you know that Fentanyl patches last a very long time and can be deadly even after being used?" Nathan had stopped working on the tray and was facing Lainey.

"Chuck simply wore protective gloves and a mask, took a couple of the used Fentanyl patches we had taken off bodies and smeared the gel from the patch onto those surfaces." He shrugged his shoulders. "As soon as Eugene began driving, he was exposed on all of the surfaces to lethal doses. It kills very rapidly. The car didn't malfunction at all. The crash happened because Eugene was already dead from the Fentanyl."

"And because you were the coroner on call, you found no evidence to order an autopsy," she said as it began to make sense to her.

"The fact that Eugene was cremated was another plus," Nathan smiled. "I figured that would be the same for Harold."

Chuck was visibly getting frustrated and nervous. "Can we shut her up now?"

Nathan looked down at Lainey as he reached for what looked like a plastic bag with pieces of paper inside. Lainey knew it was remnants of Fentanyl patches.

"But Harold died from carbon monoxide poisoning in a fish house. How did you manage that?" Lainey's eyes were wide open and focused on the patches in Nathan's hand.

Chuck answered this time. "Ann told Harold how much I liked to fish, and he said for me to come over to look at his new ritzy fish house," he stated proudly as he continued telling the story. "While he was outside getting his boat ready for storage, I looked around the fish house and smeared Fentanyl all over his fishing tackle box handle, his poles, and the knob to turn on his generator," he said. "Anything I thought he would touch."

"It was no problem for Chuck to plug the ventilation vents for the fish house after dark," Nathan chimed in. "Death by a faulty space heater and carbon monoxide is what the coroner found." He grinned. "And, of course, the coroner was me."

Nathan stopped suddenly and looked around the room. "Chuck, go into the hallway and see if someone is here. I thought I heard the service door open." Chuck nodded and went out into the hallway. He left the door standing open to the exam room.

Lainey's breath was shallow, and she knew she was running out of time. If Nathan rubbed the Fentanyl patches on her, she would be dead before anyone would find her.

Nathan, holding a small patch of gel, looked at Lainey. "Once I apply this gel on your skin, the pain will be over quickly. Don't worry, I'm sure the coroner will tell your friends you died in a horrific accident," he laughed. "Now, where should I put…"

There was a popping sound and he suddenly collapsed, falling on top of her. Lainey screamed. She saw Sarge standing in the doorway with his gun pointed at Nathan.

"Where are the patches? Did he smear them on me?" She screamed in terror.

Sarge had Nathan's body off of her and onto the floor in seconds. He frantically looked for loose scraps of patches in Nathan's hand and realized there might be some on Lainey's skin.

"Don't move Lainey!" He yelled. "I'm looking for any patches that might have fallen on you!" Lainey's heart was pounding, and she was breathing very rapidly. She tried not to move.

Finally, satisfied that no patches had touched her skin, Sarge untied her wrist and legs and helped her sit up. She crumpled into his big shoulders, scared, cold, teary-eyed, and so very thankful to be alive.

Chapter Ten

Lainey sat in the break room at the police station. She was wrapped in a blanket and sipping hot cocoa, when Francy, Vera, and Della arrived.

"Oh, my Lord, Lainey! Francy shouted as she gave her a big bear hug. "I thought you were dead!"

Vera, wiping tears from her own eyes, was hugging her, too. "Now don't you ever scare me like that again young lady!" She scolded.

Della hugged her. "Why didn't you take me with you? After all, I got you into the creamery for a tour!" She winked and added, "I know it's a crematory." They all laughed.

Sarge appeared in the doorway and smiled. "Looks like the Whoopee calvary has arrived."

"Thank you, Sarge, for saving my life. How did you

figure out where I was?" Lainey asked.

He looked at Francy. "You want to tell her?"

Francy squirmed a little bit and answered. "Remember when you left the message for me to call Sarge in an hour if I hadn't heard from you?"

"Yes and thank goodness you did!"

"Actually, I didn't get your message for several hours," Francy hesitated. "Mom and I went grocery shopping and met Della. We decided to have lunch and play a few hands of cards."

Della, Vera, and Francy all looked at Lainey, then at each other and shrugged their shoulders.

"If you were playing cards and eating, how did he know to look for me?" She asked with a puzzled look on her face.

"None of the ladies called me," Sarge confirmed.

Lainey was stunned. "What?" She sputtered. "How did you know where I was?"

"We got a search warrant for Chuck's shop and also Ann's cabin. Ann was there and not very cooperative. While my officer was searching her computer room inside the cabin, an instant message notification appeared on her screen. The message read…we're getting rid of her." Sarge leaned back in his chair.

"At the same time, I received an anonymous text message saying your car was abandoned in front of Mary's house. I took a squad with me and went straight to her house. We found your car with Mary bound and gagged in the back seat."

Lainey's eyes were glued on Sarge. Her friends were staring at him as well.

"Was Mary hurt?" Lainey asked.

Sarge shook his head no. "She was badly beaten, but the doctor says she will be fine."

There was silence in the room as everyone tried to comprehend Sarge's story.

Vera broke the silence when she said innocently, "Wish I had those honey roasted almonds I bought in the store today. I could sure use a few of them right about now!" That made everyone in the room laugh.

"Did Chuck beat up Mary and put her in my car?"

Sarge nodded. "Yes, and we found Doug bound and gagged in the trunk."

"Nathan, Chuck, and Ann were planning on killing me, Mary, and Doug by putting us in my car and making it look like an accident, weren't they?" Lainey shivered hearing her own words.

"It looks that way."

The ladies looked at each other and then back to Sarge.

"Then how in the world did you know that Chuck had taken Lainey to the county morgue?" Francy asked.

Sarge looked around the room and hesitated before responding. "I received a second anonymous text on my phone that contained two words. County morgue."

"I drove immediately to the county morgue, saw that Nathan's car and Chuck's car were there. Luckily, a deputy from the Sheriff's office had just arrived to deliver a call for a coroner to work an accident," he continued. "The outer office was dark and we heard screaming and crying coming from the back. Chuck was coming out of a door into the hallway and the deputy dropped him with his nightstick before he knew what hit him." Sarge paused. "I saw Nathan standing over you and shot him in the shoulder."

The room fell silent at the seriousness of the information, what had occurred, and how thankful they were for Sarge and his officers.

"I can never thank you enough!" Lainey said appreciatively.

He smiled and then in his semi-scolding voice said, "Next time I tell you to stop investigation something, listen to me."

She smiled and nodded. "I'll think about it!"

"Where did these anonymous text messages come from?" Francy asked. "You can trace them, can't you?"

Sarge stood and, with an odd look on his face said to Francy, "Oh, I know the source. It was from much higher up the ladder than my district." He said as he turned to leave.

"Wait!" Lainey commanded. "What higher up? Who sent those?"

"Police confidentiality, sorry." He smiled as he walked back to his office.

Lainey was back to normal after a few days' rest at home. Sarge had filled her in regarding the progress on the case. It seems in an attempt for a plea bargain, Chuck spilled his guts that Nathan and Ann were lovers and had planned to steal Doug's inheritance by murdering him and Mary. Once the DNA testing showed a link to the Sullivan fortune, the Sullivan brothers became their first targets. Chuck claimed Nathan threatened to kill him with Fentanyl patches if he didn't help them.

It was Whoopee group night and they had decided to meet at Lainey's favorite spot, Babe's House of Caffeine. She was getting ready when her phone rang. It was Raymond Sullivan.

"Hello, this is Lainey."

"Hello. This is Raymond Sullivan. Do you have a moment to speak with me?"

Her cheeks began to flush. "Sure. What can I do for you?"

"I was hoping you could meet me for dinner this evening. My car will be at your home in about twenty minutes."

She was startled for a moment. "Oh, I would love to but..." She began when he interrupted her.

"I have already cleared it with your Whoopee group. They were happy to reschedule with you."

Did he talk with the girls?

"I don't know if I appreciate your rearranging my schedule," she began slowly, "but since it appears I'm free, I would love to have dinner with you."

"That's good to hear. The car should be arriving shortly. See you soon."

She was still a bit stunned and looked at herself in her bathroom mirror. What just happened? Where are we going to eat? What do I wear? She was completely at a loss.

She hurriedly changed into her favorite black pants outfit and chose her deep purple blazer. The doorbell rang and she was greeted by a very well-dressed chauffeur who took off his hat.

"Mr. Sullivan is anxiously awaiting your arrival," he greeted.

She looked out to see a large, black limo in front of her house. *Holy cow! This will give the neighbors gossip for a month!*

Lainey thanked the gentleman and followed him to the car. He opened the door and when she got inside, she saw Raymond Sullivan sitting across from her. And he was holding two coffee cups.

"Good evening, Lainey. Thank you for dining with me on such short notice." He winked as he handed her one of the cups. "I hope you won't be disappointed, but I added a little bit of Irish Creme into our coffees this evening."

It was very rare that Lainey Maynard was left speechless. The smile on her face must have shown Raymond that she was surprised and pleased. She took her cup as he lifted his. "To a lovely evening." They touched their cups and then sipped.

"You seem to know everything about me and my dinner plans. How did you know that I was meeting with my friends tonight?"

Raymond's warm smile would have melted a hundred-year-old glacier. It certainly seemed to be melting Lainey's heart.

"I wanted to thank you for your part in apprehending the Austin brothers and for finding out the truth about Eugene's and Harold's deaths. I am forever in your debt."

"I'm very sorry about the murder of your brothers. Sarge is the one you should be thanking."

"I've been in contact with him and expressed my gratitude."

For a brief moment, Lainey saw a softness in his eyes she had not seen previously. Or, if she had, maybe she hadn't taken the time to look for it.

"You didn't answer my question, though. How did you know my schedule?" She grinned.

"I thought Sarge might have told you."

Seeing the confusion on Lainey's face, he added, "Please, let me explain."

He put his cup down, leaned forward, and took her cup from her hand. Then he clasped her hands in his.

"I hope you will not be upset, but the first time we met, you drenched me in hot coffee. I want to make sure you are unarmed now when I tell you this!" He smiled and they both laughed. He let go of her hands and sat back in his seat.

"After you came to my office to ask about Doug and Mary Reynolds, I spoke with my attorneys again concerning the possibility of my brothers being murdered." He looked out the car window and then back at her.

"They agreed to investigate further," he paused. "They decided it best to keep you under surveillance as well."

Lainey's mouth dropped open. "You had me followed?"

"Yes, but only as a precaution. I never felt you were a threat to me or my family."

She was quiet for a moment. "Your detectives or agents or whoever followed me are the ones who sent text messages to Sarge, aren't they?"

"They are undercover FBI agents, and yes, they did text Sarge about your car and they knew you had been taken to the County morgue," he said and added quickly, "I was not aware of any of this until after the arrests and your rescue had occurred. But as it turned out, I am also very grateful they followed you."

Lainey sat back, picked up her coffee cup, and took a drink. Then, looking at Raymond, she said, "I'm glad too. Thank you for having them follow me."

She reached out to take his hand in hers. Their eyes met and he leaned forward to whisper in her ear. "I would have missed having coffee spilled on me."

—————————

Keep reading for an excerpt from Murder in the Backwater *in the Lainey Maynard Mystery Series!*

Murder in the Backwater Preview

❧❦❧

For six months of the year, Mirror Falls transforms from a popular tourist vacation destination for boaters, campers, bikers, hikers, and baseball fans, into a deserted ghost town.

Old Man Winter's frigid winds, below zero temperatures, and mountains of snow force each resident into hibernation. The days when the grey sky gods allowed the sun to briefly peek its head out from among the dreary clouds could be counted on one hand. The past winter had been unusually long and bitter with more than 90 inches of the white stuff falling from October through late March.

Cabin Fever, as the locals called it, gripped every member of every household. Dogs, cats, and hamsters in town had it, too. The fever showed no mercy. Even houses felt its wrath.

Utility rooms and mud rooms were cluttered with piles of heavy down-filled coats, plaid woolen scarfs, hats and gloves, and well-worn snow boats covered with salt stains from the months of residue left on the roads. Scarred snow shovels and tired snowblowers stood in reverent silence by the garage doors, ready for action again on a moment's notice.

By the time April arrived, Cabin Fever had transformed the kindest, most even tempered of the locals into angry, impatient, caged animals chomping at the bit to escape the confines of their homes. Conversation at the local coffee shops revolved around one topic… the Minnesota Governor's Fishing Opener. It was the annual affair that kept hopes alive and locals from killing each other during the long winter.

"It's Cabin Fever, I tell you," Shep Morton said as he handed Vera the takeout food she'd ordered. "I'm getting sick and tired of cranky customers."

Vera frowned at his remark and nodded. "Oh, I know all about that. Doc referred to it as GBS… Grumpy Blues Syndrome."

"I bet he saw a bunch of angry and depressed patients. They're all crazy."

"A few of them thought he was Dear Abby! He'd have perfectly healthy patients come in and expect him to sit and listen to their complaints."

"Gossip central, that's what Doc's office was. Bet he had stories to tell you."

Vera picked up her box and turned to leave. Stopping short of the restaurant door, she turned and looked back.

"Are *you* still feuding with Charlie at the Bait Shop?"

He squinted his eyes in her direction.

"The supply committee voted to buy all the bait from him this year." Shep set his jaw and stared out the window.

"The last food committee meeting is tonight. See you there," she grinned, opened the door, and made sure it slammed shut behind her.

"Darned old goat!" she said aloud as she got into her car. "How Sally ever put up with him is beyond me."

The Whoopee group decided to meet this week at Francy's house instead of going out to one of the regular eating spots. With only a week left before the fishing opener, each was on at least one committee and needed to spend time working on various tasks. Vera had volunteered to pick up something for dinner and the ladies were sitting at the dining room table waiting for her.

Francy looked down at her watch. "Mom said she'd be here no later than 5:30. It's already 6:15. I apologize that she's late, again."

"Wasn't she going to pick up supper from the Backwater?" Lainey asked.

"Yes, and I'll bet she and Shep are wasting time arguing about something or other."

Lainey and Della looked at each other and grinned.

"What's the story, Francy?" Della asked. "Spill the beans."

"It's a ridiculous ongoing feud that started when Shep and Charlie bowled on the same team."

"Bowling?" Lainey couldn't help smiling. "In a bowling league?"

Della rested her elbows on the table. "Paul said bowling was a *big deal* back in the day."

"It was. During the winter, bowling alleys were the only places open. All of the towns around Mirror Falls had leagues and hosted tournaments," Francy said. "Women's leagues, men's leagues, mixed leagues…anything that could stand on two legs and manage to throw a bowling ball down the alley joined a league."

Lainey shook her head in amazement. "I've never heard of a bowling feud lasting fifty years. What did they argue over?"

Francy looked at the wrinkled tablecloth and grinned.

"Does Vera know, Francy?" Della asked.

"Dad might have told her."

Lainey caught the sly look between the two. "All right. Tell me what happened," she demanded.

The doorbell rang and Francy got up to answer it. Vera came inside, apologizing for being late.

"Hi, girls," she said, handing the food to Francy then

taking off her shoes and coat. "I've got comfort food…meatloaf, mashed potatoes, and gravy!"

The conversation during dinner was light and revolved around the upcoming event.

"It's your first time serving on the host board, Lainey. Is it awkward having Raymond as the chairman?" Della asked.

"You don't have to answer that, sweetie," Vera quickly chimed in. "We know it's hard for you."

Lainey twisted a piece of the tablecloth in her hands. She could feel her face flush and her entire body felt like she was in a sauna. Raymond Sullivan, the handsome CEO of the Sullivan's Best Poultry empire, had unexpectedly swept her off her feet. She hadn't dared become involved with anyone since she lost her husband. They had dated for a few months and she was happy. Until the day he called to inform her it was over.

His voice had been cold and distant. His words sharp and business like. "Lainey, you're a beautiful woman and I enjoy spending time with you. But I'm not ready for a serious relationship…"

She shivered at the memory of his voice, then tried to regain her composure.

"I don't have much contact with him," she shrugged her shoulders. "He doesn't attend many of the meetings."

"In my day, men were polite and respectful. If they

needed to talk with you, they came to your house - face to face." Vera stated. "None of this face calling or face texting or whatever it is now."

Chuckling, Francy replied, "Mom, cell phones hadn't been invented when you were dating. Guys had to find a pay phone to call you back then. And it's FaceTime, not face calling."

"We had a home phone. Besides, who had a quarter for a pay phone?" Vera asked. "Are you okay, Lainey? I'm sure he hurt your feelings."

"I'm fine working on the committee. Raymond Sullivan is past history."

How I wish I were over him!

A quiet minute passed before Della broke the silence. "The registration committee let me be the lead contact."

"You mean you got the short end of the straw when it came time to pick a chairman," Francy laughed out loud.

"Anyway," Della continued, trying hard not to smile, "I think we have five hundred entries so far. We've planned for at least twelve hundred."

"I've been studying up for the trivia contest again," Vera added. "I'm going to win that Mexico vacation package this year."

"What about Faye?" Della kidded. "Hasn't she beaten you the last several years?"

"She broke her hip in February and moved to

Florida to live with her kids," Francy grimaced. "Of course you'll beat her, Mom."

"Well, you never know. She could send in an absentee ballot!"

The laughter that followed lightened the mood and Lainey was thankful for that. She didn't want to think about Raymond.

"I do have a dilemma," Della said. "Paul tells me that the opener is politically motivated. I'm having a difficult time trying to organize who is sitting in the boat with the Governor. Any ideas?"

Francy sighed. "Politically motivated is an understatement. It's all about politics…and money."

"How so?" Lainey piped in. "Money for the city, I can see. But what makes it benefit the Governor?"

"There are only two reasons to have an official fishing opener," Vera began. "The first is for local politicians to bend the Governor's ear and get special funds for their own interests. The second is a campaign photo opportunity for his re-election bid."

"Yep. All the major news stations will follow him like a hawk," Francy agreed. "It's ridiculous the amount of dollars spent protecting the Governor so news anchors can take his picture in front of a bar holding a Minnesota craft beer."

"Channel Ten kept showing a video of him sitting behind the wheel of a big ol' green John Deere tractor last year. The wind kept blowing his straw hat off!"

Della laughed loudly. "He'd pick it up, try to pose, then it would fly off again."

Lainey rubbed her eyebrow and wrinkled her nose. "I thought it was to start the official fishing season in Minnesota."

"Oh, it is. But remember, we have more than 1.4 million licensed anglers in our state. Out of that, more than five hundred thousand will fish on opening day. And we have eighteen thousand miles of fishing streams and waters," Vera commented.

"You sound like a World Book Encyclopedia," Francy added, rolling her eyes.

"It's all in the trivia study guide. I told you, I'm going to win this year!"

"Back to my question, please," Della directed. "Whom should I put in the boat with the Governor? Can I put Democrats and Republicans in the same boat?"

Francy cleared her throat and sat up straight in her chair. "No! Only his party members in his boat. The opposing party is in the boat just behind him."

"Paul cautioned me to do that as well," Della answered.

Lainey thought she was joking. "Seriously? It's that important to keep them separate? It's just fishing, for Pete's sake."

Francy closed her eyes and nodded. "Fishing has nothing to do with."

"Years ago, Doc was in charge of the Governor's boat. Months prior to the opener, people took him out to lunch, bought him gifts, gave him tickets to sports games. They tried to bribe him to put them in the boat."

"How did he decide who got in?" Della asked.

"He put all the names in a bag, shook them up, and drew out six names."

"Well, I guess that's fair. Maybe I'll try that."

"Tell her the rest of the story, Mom."

Vera took a deep breath, then rolled her eyes. "The six whose names were drawn were happy. But twelve of those whose names weren't drawn were terribly angry. They demanded to know how he made the decision and accused him of showing partiality. When he told them he drew names out of a bag, they accused him of cheating. They demanded he hold a public drawing with the news channels present."

Della shook her head in disbelief. "That's unbelievable. What did Doc do?"

"He told them to go jump in the lake, waders and all," Vera grinned.

The friends chuckled.

"I think he later regretted his choice of words. Those twelve started a smear campaign. They spread rumors that his college internship had been falsified, that he was a drunk that was routinely seen in bars in St. Cloud, and that he had been sued for malpractice. It not only damaged his reputation, but his business suffered."

"All because Dad refused to redraw a few silly names," Francy shook her head and sighed. "It's entirely about politics."

Della's face went white. "Oh, dear. Now I know *why* they asked me to be the chairperson. I hope this doesn't do damage to Paul's reputation! What can I do?"

The group sat in silence, each one deep in thought.

"Why not let the Governor choose who he wants in the boat?" Lainey asked.

Francy rolled her eyes. "Absolutely not. He'd pick his cronies, for sure. The press would have a field day with that."

"I can see the headlines now," Vera winced. "Local Croaker's Wife Fills Governor's Boat With Hand-Picked Stink Bait."

Della shivered. "Good grief."

"Every entrant is assigned a number, correct? Well, since the purpose is to get free publicity for the Governor, why not hold a press conference and draw numbers, like a lottery," Lainey suggested.

"Hmm…" Francy said aloud. "That might work. People love lotteries. What do you think, Della?"

"If it means keeping Paul out of the line of fire, I'm all for it. I'll let the committee know tomorrow morning."

Vera sighed, clearly debating what she was about to say. "Why not hold the event at Backwater?"

The surprised look on Francy's face was unmistakable. "Mom, why are you promoting Shep's place?"

"The committee is buying all the bait from Charlie this year."

"You told Shep, didn't you?" Francy said angrily. "You know that just stirs up more trouble between him and Charlie."

Vera rolled her eyes and frowned. "Yes, I told him. So have your little ticket drawing at his place. That'll even things up."

"Vera!" Della groaned. "I'll try to persuade the committee."

As hard as she tried, Lainey couldn't stop grinning or chuckling.

"Don't you laugh," Vera said. "Shep's just a crusty old…"

"Della, I think Mom and Lainey need to be on hand for the drawing, don't you?" Francy winked.

"Oh, you better believe it. I'm not walking the plank alone!"

"Humph!" Vera grunted, crossing her arms.

———————————

Della and Lainey spent much of the next two days

organizing the press conference. What started as a small ceremony to draw names quickly snowballed into a full blown publicity event with hundreds of attendees. Suddenly, the two ladies found themselves taking orders, not giving them.

The Governor's office issued official invites. Mirror Falls dignitaries wanted to be front and center. Each of the major news stations would send crews with vans, cameras, and tons of reporters. Local law enforcement planned to beef up all security measures at the city's expense.

Della was constantly on the phone, listening to complaints or demands from the Governor's office, Sarge at the police station, and others.

Right in the middle of all the hustle and bustle was the Backwater restaurant. Shep was up in arms because the Governor's office sent a staging crew to *spruce up* the place before his arrival.

"My restaurant's been the same for forty years," Shep growled into the phone. "I don't need some politician bringing in fancy new tables and chairs."

"My hands are tied," Della tried to console him. "It's out of my control."

"They're painting the walls Chartreuse green! What kind of color is *Chartreuse green?* Looks like a darn truck stop bathroom in here!"

"Remember, all those people need to eat somewhere. It'll be a big boost to your sales."

"They'd better stay out of my kitchen! That's all I'm saying."

Della sighed as she hung up the phone. *Why did I agree to this?* she thought to herself. She was running late for a meeting with Ben Sargent and hurried to put on her coat. Before she could get into her car and pull out of her driveway, she had missed three more calls. She let them all go to voice mail.

Sarge wanted to meet at Babe's House of Caffeine to clarify his officers' roles at the press conference. As she drove to the coffee house, her Bluetooth rang. Lainey's name appeared.

"Hello?" she said hastily as she answered the call.

"Rough morning, huh?"

"It's a nightmare. It seems I'm the official complaint department!"

"Same here. I'm sorry I mentioned this press conference idea. Rose from the Governor's publicity committee called me. They told me Raymond Sullivan would be the person drawing the names."

Della didn't respond.

"He is chairman of the steering committee."

Still no response.

"It'll take the pressure off you and Paul. People will be angry with Raymond if their name isn't drawn."

"The Governor's office has taken over everything," Della said slowly.

Lainey hesitated, trying to think of the best way to phrase her reply.

"He's also going to be the Master of Ceremonies."

"They've asked him to welcome people and introduce the Governor?"

"I'm sorry, I know Paul had planned to do that."

"I see." Her voice, eerily monotone, didn't hide her disappointment.

"Francy and I are heading over to Babe's. We thought you might like a couple extra sets of ears when you meet with Sarge."

"Thanks. Maybe you can take notes for me?"

"Sure thing. We'll see you shortly."

Della disconnected the Bluetooth. She pulled into a parking space on the street in front of Babe's and turned off the car. She sat for a minute trying to gather her thoughts. She looked in the rearview mirror and wiped away the tears that had fallen. She got out of her car and headed toward the entrance.

"I've fought tougher bullies than this. They'll not get the best of this gal," she said aloud.

Sarge and Francy were waiting at a table and waved to her as she came in. She walked over, took off her coat and settled into the chair across from Sarge.

"I'm a little bit late," Della said. "I've been putting out fires." She grinned and then winked. "I'm wearing my boxing gloves…" she paused, "bring it on."

Lainey walked in the door and over to the table just

in time to hear the words *bring it on*. She saw the startled look on Sarge's face and Francy was grinning from ear to ear.

"What did I miss?" she asked as she sat down.

"What's happened? Clue me in here." Sarge looked sternly at Della and then at Francy.

"Nothing at all." Francy replied. "Regular fishing opener challenges."

Sarge shook his head and sighed. "Let's go over the logistics, Della, once more before heading over to the Backwater to start setting up. Here's a brief outline showing where our security will be, where we will setup a mobile headquarters, and the diagram for parking area barriers to be placed this afternoon."

"Why do I need this?" Della asked with a nonchalant tone in her voice. "I'm not in charge."

Sarge sat back in his chair. "We had agreed earlier that each one of you has an area to cover. Della is to make sure dignitaries are seated where they are supposed to be. Francy and one of my officers will be at the front entrance, checking credentials. Lainey is to monitor the media seating area and check press badges."

The three ladies nodded but said nothing.

He stared at Francy and Lainey for a long moment, then focused his eyes on Della. "You've heard about Sullivan."

"Put your mind at ease, Sarge," she replied casually.

"He's more than welcome to be the ringmaster for this circus." She motioned for the waitress. "Let's order lunch. I'm craving a double cheeseburger with tons of onions rings!"

Sarge shook his head and laughed. "Lunch is on me this time."

The four spent more than an hour eating lunch and planning for the next day's events.

"Time is getting away from us. I'm heading back to the station. Let's plan on meeting at Backwater in an hour. That will give my officers time to prepare."

The ladies thanked Sarge and walked out together.

"I'm proud of you, Della," Lainey said. "You handled yourself well."

"You know me. When I get pushed too far, I write the situation off. As far as I'm concerned, I'll do my assigned job, and nothing more."

"I can count on one hand the times Sarge has offered to buy lunch," Francy chuckled. "Guess it was his way of extending an olive branch."

"We've got an hour," Lainey said. "I think I'll head on over to the restaurant. I'm not too familiar with the inside and I'd like to look around before Sarge and his men arrive."

"Snoop around, you mean," Della kidded.

"That too! Where are you two headed?"

"I'm going to the funeral home first to fill in Paul. I'll meet you there."

Lainey nodded. "What about you, Francy? Wanna go with me?"

"You bet. I may need to run interference for you." She took a breath mint out of her coat pocket and popped it in her mouth.

"What's the breath mint for?" Della asked.

"Mom says Shep eats breath mints like they are going out of style. Thought I'd offer him one or two when I see him."

Lainey grinned. "Ah! Buttering him up. I like the sound of that! See you there."

The ladies hugged each other, then got in their cars.

The Backwater restaurant was a twenty-minute drive down Hwy 71 from Mirror Falls. The road wasn't normally patrolled by State Troopers, but visitors and news media caravans had flooded the area causing traffic to be heavier than usual. Troopers were positioned on both sides of the road and had cars pulled over in several spots.

Francy pulled up to the Backwater just a few seconds before Lainey. The two got out of their cars and stopped in front of the path leading to the entrance.

Lainey glanced around the area and noticed that there was only one other building nearby. She looked at Francy.

"Why in the world did they decide to have the

opener at this little spot? There's hardly enough room for our two cars to park."

"What better way for the Governor to gain favor with voters than to highlight their favorite local fishing hole. And you can be sure, he'll meet with a lot of residents and the television cameras will be rolling."

"I see. Who wouldn't want to be on the national news with the Governor?"

"Exactly. Let's go inside and find Shep."

The steppingstone path that led from the dirt parking lot to the entrance hadn't aged well. Some of the stones' corners had sunken and the winter melt had turned the grass growing between them into muddy patches, making it difficult to walk on the uneven path.

The building was a small two story house that sat thirty feet or so from the shoreline. The yellow paint had dulled over the years and a southern porch surrounded the entire place. It had once been painted white with ship plank as the railing and lattice work for decoration. A faded blue striped awning provided shade between the first and second floors. High top round tables and chairs allowed for more seating and in the summer months, a great view of the lake.

Inside, the two friends found an entourage of painters, scaffolding, and tools. The floor was completely covered in plastic and crackled when they walked on it. Somewhere a radio was blasting rock music and no one noticed they had walked inside.

"Shep?" Francy shouted as she made her way to the back of the restaurant. "Hey, Shep. It's Francy. Where are you?"

Lainey heard a loud bang and thought someone had slammed a heavy door. She saw a man wearing a white stocking cap and a stained apron making his way toward them.

"It's like a dang obstacle course in here. It's worse than KP duty in the Marines!" Shep grumbled. "Let's go out on the porch so I can hear you better."

He walked over to a set of sliding glass doors in the middle of one outside wall. He opened them, stepped onto the porch, and motioned for them to follow. He closed the door once they were outside.

"Did you bring Vera with you?"

"No, she couldn't come this time. But I know she'll be here tomorrow." Francy said smiling broadly. "This is Lainey Maynard, a friend of ours."

Lainey stepped forward and put out her hand.

"It's nice to meet you. Vera speaks highly of you." She shot a quick glance at Francy who was doing her best not to laugh.

"A Whoopee group member, I suppose. I recall reading about you in the paper," he said as he shook her hand.

Oh, great. Good old Mirror Falls gossip tabloid.

"Looks like the Backwater is getting a facelift," she commented, trying to change the subject.

His face wrinkled up causing his bushy eyebrows to almost touch each other.

"Sally and I painted this years ago. Did we paint it green? No. Do I want it painted green now? No!" He took a deep breath, then let it out slowly. "All this bunk because the *Governor* wants to *fish* here."

Lainey didn't say a word. She looked at Francy for help.

"Well, you know those darn politicians can be pushy," Francy replied. "It's a bother for sure. Maybe you'd be happier if they were painting next door at Charlie's Bait Shop instead. How about a mint?" She reached into her pocket, pulled out the container, and held it close to him.

Shep grimaced and his jaw ground back and forth on his teeth. He took the container, shook out a large handful, and shoved it back at Francy.

He popped a few mints in his mouth. "Why are you two here? The police tribe isn't supposed to show up until 4 p.m."

"We're working tomorrow and wanted to be more familiar with the building. Mind if we look around before the crowd arrives?" Lainey asked.

Shep studied their faces before he spoke. "Go ahead. I've got nothing to hide."

Nothing to hide, eh? We'll see about that.

"Thanks. We won't get in your way," Francy replied.

"Everyone is in my way. You're on your own." He

popped a few more mints into his mouth, opened the sliding door, and left them standing on the porch.

Francy smiled and looked at Lainey. "That was interesting."

"He's hiding or guarding something. We don't have much time before Sarge arrives. I'll take the kitchen and back area."

"I think I'll walk over to Charlie's. It gives me an excuse to look around the outside."

Lainey opened the door and walked toward the kitchen. The painters were cleaning up and didn't notice her. She found the door to the kitchen and went inside. It wasn't a big space and she was surprised how clean it looked considering the work being done in the front. She looked around for Shep but saw no one.

She walked through the cooking area, opening cabinets and closets, and found nothing but supplies and utensils. There were two tall freezers on one wall that had locks on their door handles. She noticed a hallway just to the left of them. She looked back to make sure no one was in the room and then walked down the hallway. There was a bathroom on one side and a maintenance room on the other. At the end of the hallway was a door with the words *Shep and Sally* stenciled on it in black paint.

Lainey put her ear to the door to see if she could hear anyone inside. When she heard nothing, she tried opening it. It was locked. She reached into her fanny pack, took out her credit card, and started to work on opening the lock.

"Glad I had to watch those videos using credits cards to open locks. Let's hope this works," she said aloud.

After a couple of tries, the door unlocked. She looked behind her quickly, then opened the door and went inside. She found the light switch, flipped it on, and closed the door. She expected it to be an office or something similar. Instead, she saw a small kitchen complete with a standing oven, double sink, a refrigerator, and some sort of island or chopping station. And hanging from a wooden rack beside the fridge were strands of dried-up fish entrails. Some of the skeletons still had skin on them.

Why would he have a kitchen inside his regular kitchen?

Her cell phone pinged signaling a text had come in. She quickly took her phone out of her fanny pack and read the text from Francy.

"Sarge is pulling in the parking lot."

Lainey quickly snapped a picture of the room with her phone. She opened the door and turned off the light. She reset the lock and shut the door, testing it to make sure it was locked.

She hurried back through the kitchen and into the dining room just as Sarge and his men were walking in. She was walking toward them when a man's voice from behind startled her. She stopped and turned around to see Shep glaring at her.

"Find what you were looking for?"

"Yes, you have a beautiful kitchen area. I'm looking forward to tasting your cooking tomorrow."

"I didn't hire you to cook. It gets really hot in my kitchen. Stay out or you might get burned."

She nodded and turned back around.

You might be surprised just how hot it can get.

———————————————

WANT TO JOIN LAINEY AND HER FRIENDS ON THEIR NEXT adventure, Murder In The Backwater? Click the link below!

Murder In the BackWater

——————————

And now for your free ebook!

https://dl.bookfunnel.com/d82s2jng1p

An Excerpt from Roommates:

She has a bossy Siamese cat and needs a new roommate...

He has a slobbering bulldog and needs a place to stay...

Changing her dreams of buying a red Mercedes convertible after college is something Lainey Bonner didn't want to do. Her senior year, she and her best friend, Amy, had signed a rental lease for a house instead of living on campus. They had agreed to split the rent and utilities. Lainey's cat, Angel, loved Amy and the first semester worked out perfectly... until Christmas break.

From the moment Amy announced she would be moving out and had arranged for a guy to move in, Lainey realized her dreams were in jeopardy. Facing the possibility of paying the full amount of rent for the remainder of the lease weighed heavily on her, not to mention the fact that some strange guy with a bulldog was moving in.

When she met Darren Maynard, his crooked smile and dimple made her tingle all over. He was intelligent with an easy-going personality that made him almost adorable. Lainey's keen intuition had guided her in the past, but the thought of living with a handsome engineer and his slobbering bulldog worried her. Could the animals get along? What would her Dad say?

———————————————

December 1, School of Mines and Technology, Rapid City, SD

The shock on Lainey's face was obvious. She was stunned at the bombshell her college roommate, Amy Walker, had just dropped in her lap.

"I'm pregnant and moving out as soon as the semester is over," Amy stated happily.

"Wait. What? You're moving out?" Lainey stuttered.

"Yep. Bubba and I are so happy!"

What? Who is Bubba? Moving out? I'm stuck with the rental lease?

Lainey sat slowly in the old green recliner she had purchased at a flea market last semester. Her mind was running a mile a minute. She and Amy had agreed last summer to rent this house together to finish out their senior year at the School of Mines. The old, run down house on Quincy Street was nothing to write home about. But it was close to the campus and gave Lainey privacy she couldn't get in her old dorm room in Connolly Hall. They had agreed to split the rent and utilities and had signed a one year lease with the landlord.

"I know it's a shock," Amy began. "Bubba's dad is going to let him work in his Caterpillar dealership repairing engines and big stuff like that."

"But it's your senior year. You're so close to graduation. You're going to give that all up?"

"Oh, I didn't really like engineering anyway.

Bubba's going to make loads of money and I can stay home and raise little Bubba babies. Isn't that just dreamy?" Amy excitedly giggled.

Lainey shook her head in disbelief. Images of her being forced to work double shifts at Spuds and Stuff and watching the world gather at the clock in the center of Rushmore Mall by Osco Drug made her shudder.

"We signed a year lease for this house," Lainey muttered. "I can't afford to pay for this by myself."

"Don't you worry about that," Amy casually responded as she read a text on her phone. "Bubba's dad has a friend whose son goes here. He's moving in this weekend."

Lainey was speechless...again. Her mouth was open, but no words came out. Her seal point Siamese cat, Angel, jumped in her lap and appeared to sneer in Amy's direction.

Amy finished texting, looked at Angel and smiled.

"And it gets better...he has the cutest little doggie you've ever seen. Angel will simply love him!"

———————————————

It was snowing heavily as Lainey left the Mechanical Engineering building and walked across the Quad toward the Surbeck Student Center. Amy's recent departure and the anticipation of sharing her space with some guy she had never met set her nerves on edge. She hadn't been able to concentrate or study for her last final in Fluid Mechanics as much as she wanted to. After grabbing a coffee at the Miners Shack, she headed over to the library to study a bit more.

Many of the students had already gone home for Christmas break. Lainey planned to stay in Rapid and work through the holidays. She could pick up extra shifts and sock money away for the graduation present she intended to give herself... A red Mercedes convertible. Her passion for convertibles began when her dad traded a bunch of old pipe valves for a 1967 yellow and black Chevy Camaro convertible. It was her first car and while it was a junker, she thought she was riding in style!

The previous owner had stripped the car down to rebuild it as a race car. Needless to say the work was shoddy and about half complete. When her dad parked the car in the driveway, Lainey couldn't wait to get behind the wheel and drag Main Street. She didn't notice the faded yellow paint job, the dents and dings, the crooked antenna on the driver's side, or the words *Hanky Panky* on a sticker on the door. Little did she know that the car would be the source of some of her most embarrassing memories.

It had bucket seats. The driver's side seat was a dingy black and white plaid fabric. The passenger seat was covered with what looked like orange shag carpet that had clumped in places. It was a 4-speed and the shifter in between the bucket seats was a tall, thick piece of metal covered half-way up from the floorboard with what looked like the bottom of a rubber toilet bowl plunger. The top was graced with a large chrome ball that had a smiley face carved or chiseled into it.

Lainey's inaugural trip down Main Street didn't go as she had planned. After spending more than ten minutes getting the car started, plugging in an Elton John 8-track tape in the used player her dad had installed where the radio should have been, and using both hands to crank down the rusted driver's side window, she was ready to show off her new wheels.

Main Street was about three miles from her house. She rested her left elbow on the open window door frame, keeping her hand on the steering wheel when she shifted gears and put her foot on the gas. Her tires squealed and she was in heaven. Until she looked in the rearview mirror to see the flashing red lights behind her. She pulled over. She had gone less than a mile.

Flustered, she forgot to hold the clutch in before she turned off the engine and the car lurched forward, jerking to stop. She heard a familiar voice coming from her open driver's window.

"Got a new car, Lainey?"

She sighed, rolled her eyes, and shrugged her shoulders.

"Hello, Lt. Garrett," Lainey answered sheepishly. He happened to be the chairman of the board of elders at her church and great friends with her parents.

"Were you planning on dragging Main?"

"Yes, sir," she sighed.

"Did you happen to hear anything odd as you were burning rubber when you took off?"

Lainey knew that she had the volume on the 8-track turned as high as it would go…and she figured he knew that too.

"No, sir."

"Elton was singing pretty loudly, wasn't he?"

She nodded her head yes.

"Please step out of the car. I want to show you something."

Lainey got out of the car and slowly followed the officer to the back of her car.

"See anything strange here?"

She swallowed hard and nodded yes.

"And what do you see?"

"I think it's the tailpipe."

"Is it supposed to be dragging the ground? Or smoking? Or throwing sparks as it digs holes in the pavement?"

Lainey had no idea that the tailpipe in question had been loosely attached to the car with a thin piece of chicken wire. Since her driveway was made of pea gravel, when she squealed her tires, the rocks thrown up knocked the pipe loose. It had been dragging behind her the entire time. The crooked carved line left behind in the hot pavement was evidence of that.

When Lt. Garrett had thoroughly embarrassed and scolded her, she slid behind the wheel, and headed home to face her dad. Before the officer could walk to his car, a loud, high pitched, screeching sound pierced the air. He slowly walked back to the Camaro.

Lainey was frantically pushing the middle of the racing steering wheel trying to stop the sound. She didn't even know the car *had* a horn. Nothing was happening. The sound continued to blare. Officer Garrett got in the car and tried to turn it off. Nothing.

Lainey was mortified, sitting beside the road, police car lights flashing behind her, and horn blasting while her classmates drove past. Some were waving, some were laughing, and some drove past a few times. The dreadful horn sounded until her dad arrived and unplugged it from under the dashboard. It would be a long time before she'd live this down.

From that point on, she had decided to never again be embarrassed by a junkyard automobile. She'd save her money and as a reward for getting her college degree, she'd buy a red Mercedes convertible.

But now that plan might be in jeopardy. Facing the possibility of having to pay the full amount of rent for the remainder of the lease was weighing heavily on her, not to mention the fact that some strange guy was planning on moving in with her.

"I can't tell my dad a guy is moving in with me. He'll have a fit," Lainey said aloud as she walked to her favorite spot in the library. This little nook and table had become her home-away-from-home the last four years. She spent more time here than in her dorm room. The library workers knew her by name and referred to that spot as *Bonner's Cell.*

Lainey laid her backpack on the left corner of the small table and put her coffee cup on the right. It made it easy for her to grab different textbooks, pencils, and notebooks from the backpack and not spill her coffee. She had been known to spill a few drops here or there.

"How's the java today, Lainey? I thought the Shack would be closed for Christmas break," a familiar male voice teased.

Jess Martin was also a business management technology major. Since their freshman year, they had been in every core class together. He helped her through Statistics, she helped him with Communications and Writing. Lainey thought he might have had a little crush on her that first year and while he was nice, kind, and cute, she was determined to focus on getting her degree with no strings attached to anyone. She explained to him that she wasn't looking for a relationship in the kindest way possible.

He was disappointed at first, but since that day, they had become good friends.

"I have the caffeine-addicts preferred service at the Shack. They wouldn't dare close until after my last final!"

The two chuckled. Lainey stood up to take off her old winter coat and immediately began struggling with the worn out zipper.

"I swear, the teeth on this zipper are as jagged as the smile on a pumpkin's face!" she complained.

She threw up her arms in frustration, knocking her beloved coffee cup into the air.

It was like watching in slow motion as Jess leaned forward to try to catch the flying beverage and instead, tackling some poor student who happened to be walking by. Jess and the unlucky student fell to the ground and the cup poured out its contents on them as if it were on purpose.

"Oh!" Lainey exclaimed. "I'm so sorry! Are you both okay?"

"I'm okay, but Darren might not be. He broke my fall," Jess replied, standing up and offering a hand to help.

"Thanks, but I'm fine," the guy said, motioning off Jess's hand. He stood up and looked down at the wet spots on his jeans. "Nice tackle. What's this wet stuff anyway?"

"It's my coffee," Lainey said. "I was trying to get my

zipper unstuck and knocked my cup off the table. Here, let me clean it up." She riffled through her coat pockets, pulled out a couple of crumpled napkins, and started to pat the spots on Darren's jeans. He jerked back in surprise, taking the napkins out of her hand.

"Hey…what are you doing?" Darren sputtered uneasily. He glanced at Jess, then at Lainey who was obviously embarrassed.

"I'm sure you can wipe yourself…uhm…it's not like I felt your leg or… I mean, you can pat yourself dry… oh, golly," she sighed aloud, horrified at how ridiculous her words sounded.

"Lainey was trying to help, that's all," Jess laughed. "She's the queen of klutz when it comes to coffee."

Darren rolled his eyes and walked away. "See you, Jess."

Lainey looked at Jess who was still laughing.

"Stop grinning and giggling! He thinks I'm an idiot!"

"Nah, he probably thinks you're a first semester freshman who doesn't have a clue," Jess chuckled. "That was vintage Lainey for sure."

"Humph." Lainey glared at him. "Who was that guy? I haven't seen him around."

"His name is Darren Maynard. He's a mechanical engineering major and has the brains of an Einstein. He's a senior, too."

"No wonder he can't carry on a decent conversation. Those ME's can play with numbers, but the few I know aren't very good at socializing, unless it's beer chugging and wet tee shirt contests over at the Hall."

Jess laughed. "When's your exam?"

"Ten-thirty this morning," she responded, sitting down and reorganizing her table. "I've been so stressed about Amy moving out and how I'm going to pay the rent, I'm not as prepared as I should be."

"You got this. MacDonald's final is predictable. He takes questions from the previous exams, mostly those missed by the class, and rewords them. You'll do fine. He knows what a good student you are."

Lainey shrugged. "I sure hope so. I need this class and a good grade on my transcript."

"I'll call you later," Jess said as he winked at her. "I'm heading home this afternoon."

"Sounds good."

She studied for a solid hour, then headed back across the Quad to her class for the exam. She dreaded timed tests. She usually knew most of the answers, but would get flustered trying to watch the clock to make sure she hadn't spent more than one minute on each question.

She had a routine of reading the first question and the last question. If she knew the answers to those, her stress level went down. If not, she knew it would be a race against the clock. Luckily, she knew them both today.

Thank you, Lord! Help me remember what I know and pass this test!

She put the completed test on Prof. MacDonald's desk with a few minutes to spare.

"Finished early, Lainey?" He asked, looking up through his thick framed glasses that were perched on his nose.

"Just a couple of minutes early," she said smiling.

"Perhaps I didn't make it hard enough then." He teased.

"No, no, it was more than adequate! I hope you have a Merry Christmas, sir."

"You, too. Grades will be posted by end of the day."

Lainey nodded and walked out of the classroom. She liked Professor MacDonald and was sorry this was her last class with him. She hurried across campus to her car and found a note taped to the windshield. It was from Amy.

I'm all moved out and here is my new phone number. Your new roomie is moving in this evening. I'll miss you!

Lainey gave a huge sigh as she got in her car.

Already? I still don't know who this guy is?

She started the car and headed to the grocery store to purchase milk and cat food. She was in and out quickly and headed to her house. Her mind wasn't on driving or grocery shopping or Christmas. It was clearly focused on who this roommate was and how she was going to explain him to her dad.

As she pulled into her regular parking spot on the street in front of the house, she noticed the side door was open. She grabbed her backpack and grocery bag, locked her car, and headed for the open door. She was worried that Angel had gotten out.

Why would Amy leave the door open?

She hurried inside, putting her stuff on the counter, and closed the door.

"Angel? Angel kitty? Where are you, sweetie?" Lainey called out, searching for the Siamese cat.

She heard a loud growling coming from her bedroom and knew it was Angel's angry sound.

Lainey couldn't have been more surprised by what she found in her bedroom. Angel, back raised up, tail fluffed out wide, was clawing and growling at a small wire kennel that held something captive in it.

"Angel, stop. It's okay." She picked up the territorial feline. "What are you growling at?"

Bending down, Lainey could see a dog in the back of the metal kennel. It was cowering, shaking...and slobbering.

"What in the world? It's okay, little fella. Angel won't hurt you." She put the cat in the hallway, closed the bedroom door to keep her out for a minute, and opened the kennel to try and urge the dog out. He slowly inched forward, sniffing and whimpering, until she could pet him.

"You're okay," she said, picking him up while trying

not to get his slobber all over herself. She grabbed a tissue to clean his face. He was a pudgy little tan and white bulldog with so many wrinkles around his mouth that made him look adorable. "Why, you're a little cutie!" She wiped his face off and he seemed to calm down a bit.

Angel had been scratching and meowing loudly at the closed door, trying to get in. Lainey, still holding the bulldog, opened the door. The cat ran inside, made a beeline to the open kennel door, and sneaked inside to see where the dog was hiding.

"He's not in there, Angel," Lainey said, watching the bulldog begin to pant. "What's your name, little fella?"

"His name is Brutus," a male voice boomed out, startling Lainey.

She turned to see who it was. Her mouth fell open and she almost dropped the dog.

"You? How did you get..." Lainey began, then suddenly realized what was happening.

"You're the new roommate, aren't you. And this is your dog," she said with resignation in her voice.

"You must be Amy's old roommate. And that cat must be yours," the guy replied, not amused. "Any plans to spill coffee on me in the next few minutes?"

Just as Lainey was about to speak, the cute little bulldog she was holding let out the loudest, stinkiest toot she had ever heard or smelled.

"Oh, my gosh!" Lainey yelled, quickly handing the

dog to its owner and covering her nose. "That smells terrible!"

"He passes gas when he gets nervous," the guy grinned widely. "I'll take him outside for a minute."

He patted the dog. As he turned to take him outside, he said softly, but loud enough he was sure Lainey could hear. "Good boy, Brutus. Show her who's boss."

"Humph!" she exclaimed disgustedly. She turned to Angel who had gotten out of Brutus's kennel and was standing guard next to her leg. "He *thinks* he's the boss, does he? We'll just see about that!" She bent down, picked up Angel, and stormed back into the kitchen.

You can make a big difference!

If you've enjoyed my book, please leave a review!

Reviews are the most important and powerful ways to spread the word about my books.

I believe I have something more effective and personal than any type of ad.

It's you! Building a relationship with committed and loyal readers is powerful!

An honest review will help bring my books to other readers, something no amount of advertising can accomplish!

I humbly and gratefully ask you to spend a few minutes leaving a review if you enjoyed my book. It can be as short or long as you like.

Thank you and blessings on your day!

Please leave a review! The Family Tree Murders

Acknowledgements

Writing stories, creating characters, and completing a novel or series involves many people. I humbly want to thank all who helped or listened to my questions, rants and insecurities during this process!

First, to my family for their enduring patience while I spent hours and days peering at my computer screen. You have my utmost thanks and love. Contrary to your general consensus, I did stop long enough to eat and shower. A special thanks to my son, Aaron, and Officer Dustin Vanderhagen, a BCA special agent, for their expertise and collaboration in law enforcement situations. I will not soon forget our chats concerning morgues, retorts, and autopsies.

Thank you to my editor, Grace Augustine, and my publisher/book cover designer, Linda Boulanger. Your talents, patience, and kindness gave me inspiration and determination. I look forward to many more projects with you both!

Thank you to all those who volunteered to read and review this book prior to its release. Your input was invaluable.

Thank you to the successful authors and writers who so kindly provided helpful insights to their past experiences.

Lastly, thank you to Alvina, Carol, Dawn, Debbie, and Marie. Our dinners, game nights, and adventures over the years have meant so much to me. You stood by me with hugs, encouragement, friendship and gave me reasons to laugh when I thought I couldn't. You are my extended family and I love you all.

To readers, I hope you enjoy this first book in the Lainey Maynard Mystery series and will follow her coming adventures! To get pre-order specials, release date previews and more, go to LauraHern.com and use your email to signup.

Blessings to you always!

Laura Hern

Have You Heard?

Get Laura Hern's Newest Previews and Preorder Launch Specials Now!

www.laurahern.com

Sign up for the latest news on previews, special offers, and preorder information for the Lainey Maynard Mystery Series and more.

About the Author

Laura Hern writes cozy mysteries and romantic comedy. This is her third book in The Lainey Maynard Mystery series.

Her website is www.laurahern.com.

You can connect with Laura on her author Facebook page, on Twitter, and her website.

Also by Laura Hern

Murder in the Backwater

Curtain Call at Brooksey's Playhouse

Christmas Corpse At Caribou Cabin

and more coming soon!

Made in the USA
Columbia, SC
24 November 2024

47016549R00129